Welcome to Penhally Bay!

Nestled on the rugged Cornish coast is the picturesque town of Penhally. With sandy beaches, breathtaking landscapes and a warm, bustling community—it is the lucky tourist who stumbles upon this little haven.

But now Mills & Boon® Medical™ Romance is giving readers the unique opportunity to visit this fictional coastal town through our brand-new twelve-book continuity... You are welcomed to a town where the fishing boats bob up and down in the bay, surfers wait expectantly for the waves, friendly faces line the cobbled streets and romance flutters on the Cornish sea breeze...

We introduce you to Penhally Bay Surgery, where you can meet the team led by caring and commanding Dr Nick Tremayne. Each book will bring you an emotional, tempting romance—from Mediterranean heroes to a sheikh with a guarded heart. There's royal scandal that leads to marriage for a baby's sake, and handsome playboys are tamed by their blushing brides! Top-notch city surgeons win adoring smiles from the community, and little miracle babies will warm your hearts. But that's not all...

With Penhally Bay you get double the reading pleasure... as each book also follows the life of damaged hero Dr Nick Tremayne. His story will pierce your heart—a tale of lost love and the torment of forbidden romance. Dr Nick's unquestionable, unrelenting skill would leave any patient happy in the knowledge that she's in safe hands, and is a testament to the ability and dedication of all the staff at Penhally Bay Surgery. Come in and meet them for yourself...

Dear Reader

I was delighted when my editor invited me to take part in an exciting new series for Medical™ Romance based in the fictitious town of Penhally, in North Cornwall. As many readers know, Cornwall has always been a favourite setting of mine, and when I was asked to tell the story of a delicious Italian hero I couldn't wait to get started!

Marco Avanti is a super-sexy Italian doctor with a special interest in paediatrics. He's strong and commanding, and the object of all the local women's fantasies, but he isn't interested in romance because he is still in love with just one woman—his wife, Amy, who walked out on him two years previously.

But Marco is about to receive a shock. Amy arrives unannounced in his surgery on a cold, snowy morning between Christmas and New Year, and she is asking for a divorce. *Will he let her go a second time?*

I loved developing the character of Marco, because he possesses all the qualities I expect from a hero. He is strong, skilled at his job, confident and passionate, but he also has a gentle side and is determined to protect those he loves.

2008 is the year of Mills & Boon's one hundredth birthday, so it seems especially appropriate to have contributed to a series that required such close collaboration. It was wonderful to have this chance to work with so many of the other medical authors and the talented team of editors at Harlequin Mills and Boon. I know that Penhally Bay and its inhabitants came to life for all of us, and hopefully we've created something really special for you to enjoy.

Warmly

Sarah

x

THE ITALIAN'S NEW-YEAR MARRIAGE WISH

BY
SARAH MORGAN

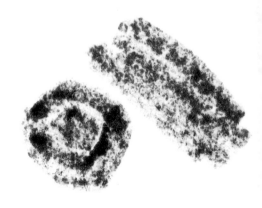

MILLS & BOON®

Pure reading pleasure

**To Sheila Hodgson, for all the support and encouragement.
Thank you.**

First published in Great Britain 2007
Harlequin Mills & Boon Limited,
Eton House, 18-24 Paradise Road, Richmond, Surrey TW9 1SR

Set in Times Roman 10½ on 12¼ pt
15-1107-53937

Printed and bound in Great Britain
by Antony Rowe Ltd, Chippenham, Wiltshire

Sarah Morgan trained as a nurse, and has since worked in a variety of health-related jobs. Married to a gorgeous businessman, who still makes her knees knock, she spends most of her time trying to keep up with their two little boys, but manages to sneak off occasionally to indulge her passion for writing romance. Sarah loves outdoor life, and is an enthusiastic skier and walker. Whatever she is doing, her head is always full of new characters and she is addicted to happy endings.

BRIDES OF PENHALLY BAY
Bachelor doctors become husbands and fathers—
in a place where hearts are made whole

At Christmas we met pregnant doctor Lucy Tremayne
when she was reunited with the man she loves
Christmas Eve Baby by Caroline Anderson

This January enjoy some much needed winter warmth
with gorgeous Italian doctor Marco Avanti
The Italian's New-Year Marriage Wish by Sarah Morgan

Then join Adam and Maggie in February
on a 24-hour rescue mission where romance
begins to blossom as the sun starts to set
The Doctor's Bride by Sunrise by Josie Metcalfe

Single dad Jack Tremayne finds a mother for his little
boy—and a bride for himself this March
The Surgeon's Fatherhood Surprise by Jennifer Taylor

There's a princess in Penhally! HRH Melinda Fortesque
comes to the Bay in April
The Doctor's Royal Love-Child by Kate Hardy

Edward Tremayne finds the woman of his dreams in May
Nurse Bride, Bayside Wedding by Gill Sanderson

Meet hunky Penhally Bay Chief Inspector Lachlan D'Ancey
and follow his search for love this June
Single Dad Seeks a Wife by Melanie Milburne

The temperature really hots up in July when devastatingly
handsome Dr Oliver Fawkner arrives in the Bay…
Virgin Midwife, Playboy Doctor by Margaret McDonagh

Curl up with Francesca and Mark in August as they
try one last time for the baby they've always longed for...
Their Miracle Baby by Caroline Anderson

September brings sexy Sheikh Zayed
from his desert kingdom to the beaches of Penhally
Sheikh Surgeon Claims His Bride by Josie Metcalfe

Snuggle up with dishy Dr Tom Cornish in October
A Baby for Eve by Maggie Kingsley

And don't miss French doctor Pierre,
who sweeps into the Bay this November
Dr Devereux's Proposal by Margaret McDonagh

A collection to treasure for ever!

CHAPTER ONE

'I WANT a divorce, I want a divorce, I want a divorce…'

Amy recited the words in her head as the taxi wound its way along the small country roads that led towards the North Cornish coast. The snow that had fallen overnight had dusted fields, trees and bushes with a wintry layer of white that now glistened and sparkled under the bright early morning sunshine. It promised to be a perfect day—perfect for people who weren't about to end their marriage.

She felt sicker than she'd ever felt in her life and the brief glimpse of the sea in the distance increased the tension in her stomach until it felt as though she'd swallowed a loop of knotted rope. No amount of logical reasoning or deep breathing produced the desired feeling of calm and suddenly Amy wished she hadn't chosen to come in person. But what else could she have done when he'd refused to respond to her letters or phone calls?

He'd left her no choice.

Staring out of the window at the familiar landmarks, she admitted to herself that his protracted silence had surprised her. It was so unlike him. He was Italian after all, and she'd braced herself for an ongoing display of simmering, volcanic passion.

Marco was single-minded and determined. A man who knew what he wanted from life and took it.

Which just went to prove that he clearly hadn't wanted her.

Amy felt her throat close and she swallowed hard, controlling the tears, aware that she was being completely illogical. It wasn't as if she'd *wanted* him to put up a fight. It would have made it so much harder to do what had to be done.

Amy curled her hands tightly over the edge of her seat. She wanted to tell the taxi driver to turn round and take her back to the station but she knew that she couldn't give in to that impulse. If she didn't do this now then she'd only have to do it later and she'd already put it off as long as possible.

It was time to finally end their marriage.

She was so lost in thought that it took a moment for her to realise that the taxi driver was speaking to her. 'I'm sorry? Did you say something?'

The taxi driver glanced in his mirror. 'Just wondering if you live in Penhally.'

Amy managed a polite smile. 'No.' She consciously relaxed her hands. 'Not any more. I used to, before…' *Before her entire life had fallen apart.* 'I lived here for a while.'

'So…' He drove carefully down a road still white with snow. 'I expect you're home to celebrate New Year with your family? Are you staying long?'

No family. No celebrations.

'It's just a short visit,' she said huskily. 'I'm here until this evening. My train is at eight o'clock.'

Which left her just enough time to confront her husband and say, 'I want a divorce.' And then she would never see Penhally again.

'Well, keep an eye on the weather. Can you believe that it snowed again last night? I mean, when did we last have snow like this on the coast? When was it last this cold?' He shook his head. 'Global warming, that's what it is. Our entire climate has gone bonkers. And there are severe storms forecast. Leave plenty of time or you'll find yourself stranded and miss that train.'

Barely listening, Amy glanced out of the window. She'd be leaving Penhally that evening even if it meant walking.

As the taxi turned into the main street, her heart rate doubled, as if her body was instinctively bracing itself for conflict.

She slid down slightly in her seat and then frowned with exasperation and sat up again. *What was she doing?* She was behaving like a fugitive, not a thirty-five-year-old doctor with a responsible career!

But the thought of actually seeing Marco again shredded her self-control, confidence and dignity into tiny pieces. For the past two years she'd dreamed about him, thought about him and cried about him. No matter what she'd been doing, he'd dominated her thoughts, but she'd spared herself the torture of actually bumping into him by taking herself as far away as possible.

Unable to trust herself not to weaken, she hadn't just left the village or the country—she'd left the continent.

'Stop here.' Suddenly anxious that she might bump into Marco before she was ready to see him, she leaned forward. 'Thank you, this is perfect. I can walk from here.' She fumbled in her bag for her purse, paid the taxi driver and slid out of the back of the car, clutching her small bag.

She waited for the taxi to pull away and stood for a moment, staring down the main street of Penhally. It was still too early for the shops to open but Christmas lights twinkled in the windows and decorations glittered and winked. The addition of snow produced a scene that could have been taken straight from a Dickens novel and Amy gave a tiny smile, suddenly feeling more Christmassy than she had over Christmas itself. Memories slid into her head: memories of walking hand in hand with her grandmother, choosing decorations for the Christmas tree; collecting the turkey from the butcher.

She'd always thought that Penhally was a magical place.

Her few happy childhood memories were centred on this Cornish fishing village.

She'd wanted her own children to grow up here.

'Amy? Amy Avanti?'

The voice came from directly behind her and she turned, her palms damp with sweat and her heart pounding frantically against her chest. It was as if she'd been caught shoplifting instead of just returning home unannounced.

'Tony…' She managed a smile even though she was secretly wishing that the landlord of the Smugglers' Inn hadn't chosen this particular moment to walk up the street. 'You're up early.'

'Busy time of year.' The collar of his coat was turned up against the winter chill as he studied her face, a question in his eyes. 'So that's it? I haven't seen you for ages and all you can say is, "You're up early"?'

'Sorry.' Feeling suddenly awkward, Amy huddled deeper into her coat. 'I suppose I don't really know what to say…'

'You always were a woman who listened more than you spoke…' Tony grinned '…which makes a pleasant change. Does Marco know you're home?'

'No.' *She hadn't wanted him forewarned.* Her only hope was to catch him off guard. She was banking on the fact that he'd be so shocked to see her that he wouldn't say much. *Wouldn't make things difficult.* 'It was an impulse thing. We have things to discuss.'

'Well, I heard the Maserati roaring down the street earlier so he's probably already at the surgery. They're busy over there.'

His words brought a disturbingly vivid memory to life. A memory of a hot summer's day two and a half years before when she and Marco had just arrived in Penhally, newly married and full of plans. *Full of hope and optimism.* Marco had taken her for a ride in his beloved Maserati, a car that perfectly matched his testosterone-driven approach to life. He'd driven the car along the coast road, one hand on the wheel, the other laid possessively over the back of her seat, and Amy had been so madly and crazily in love with him that she'd spent the entire trip gazing in disbelief at his profile.

And he'd guessed how she'd felt, of course, because he was a man who knew women and his cool sophistication and greater life experience had just increased her own, deep-seated insecurity.

Why was he with her?

How many times had she asked herself that question? Amy swallowed hard and pushed the thought away. He *wasn't* with her. Not any more. And although it had been her decision, she knew that by leaving she'd simply hastened the inevitable. 'I'm surprised he's driving the Maserati. It always hated cold weather.'

'It still hates cold weather. Last week it died by the side of the road and your husband was gesticulating and letting out a stream of Italian. The entire village was in the bookshop looking up words in the Italian dictionary but we all know that when it comes to his precious car, Marco doesn't always use words that are in the dictionary.' Tony scratched his head. 'I suggested he buy a traditional English car designed to cope with traditional English weather, but he treated that suggestion with the contempt that it probably deserved.'

'I can imagine he wasn't enthusiastic.'

'It's good to see you back, Amy. We were surprised when you went.'

'Yes.' She had no doubt that she'd left the entire village reeling with shock. Marco Avanti just wasn't a man that women left, especially not a plain, ordinary woman like her, who should have been grateful to have attracted the attention of anyone, let alone an Italian heartthrob.

And she hadn't offered an explanation.

How could she? It had all been too personal, too private. *Too devastating.*

'Well, it's good to see you home, even if it's only for a short time. If you hurry, you'll catch Marco before he starts surgery. He's pretty busy. I expect you heard about Lucy? She had her baby early and so now they're a doctor down.'

Were they?

She hadn't had news of Penhally for a year, not since that one, solitary letter she'd received from Kate Althorp, the practice manager, who had once been her friend.

'They must be busy.' Which made it better for her. Marco wouldn't have time to argue or make things difficult. She was going to walk into the surgery, say what needed to be said and then leave before he had time to compose arguments. Hopefully he'd be too wrapped up in the needs of his patients to be particularly bothered about an almost ex-wife.

Amy shivered slightly, her breath leaving clouds in the freezing air. 'I'll see you later, Tony.'

'Make sure you do. Pop into the Smugglers' for a drink before you leave.'

'Yes.' She smiled, knowing that she wouldn't. What was the point of exposing herself to gossip for the sake of one drink when the entire liquid contents of the pub wouldn't be enough to dull the pain of seeing Marco Avanti again?

At the other end of the village in the state-of-the-art GP surgery that served the local community, Marco Avanti lounged in his chair, staring with brooding concentration at the computer screen on his desk. 'Kate?' he called through the open door. 'Didn't you say that the blood results for Lily Baxter had come through?'

'We haven't had time to enter them on the system yet.' Kate walked into the room, carrying a mug of coffee. 'With Lucy going on early maternity leave, we've been concentrating on finding a locum. Being one doctor down over the Christmas period just doesn't work. I found four more grey hairs when I woke up this morning.' She moved a stack of journals and put the coffee on his desk. 'Here, drink this. You're going to need it. It's going to take you until this evening to get through the amount of patients booked in today.'

The pungent, seductive aroma of fresh coffee filled the air and Marco gave an appreciative groan. 'You made that for me? Truly, you're an angel, *amore*.' He curled long, strong fingers around the mug and lifted it, the smell penetrating the clouds of tiredness that threatened to fog his brain. '*Tutto bene*? Everything OK? Tell me the worst. The village has been consumed by an attack of cholera? Plague? Everyone is queuing to see me, no?'

'Don't even joke about it. And as for the queue…' Kate smiled wearily. 'You don't want to know. Just take them one at a time and if you're still here tonight, I'll bring you a sleeping bag.'

'Just make sure the sleeping bag contains a warm, willing woman,' he drawled, and Kate smiled.

'You're incorrigible.' She moved towards the door and Marco put the mug on his desk.

'Did you find time to call the garage about the Maserati?'

'Yes. They're coming in a minute to see to it. Give me the keys and then I won't have to disturb you.'

Grateful that there was one less thing that he had to manage, Marco reached into the pockets of the coat that he'd thrown over the back of the chair and tossed her the keys. 'Here. *Grazie*, Kate. Not only are you *molto belissima*, you are also efficient.'

'It's called time management. If I sort out your car, then you spend more time with patients. It's a solution that works for everyone, so you don't need to waste your Italian charm on me.'

'Why is it a waste?' Enjoying the brief distraction of mean-ingless banter, Marco leaned back and gave her a slow smile. 'Run away with me, Kate. We could both leave this cold, windy place and live in sin in my beautiful Italy. I own a *palazzo* in Venice, right on the edge of the canal.' He watched as a shadow flickered across her eyes.

Then she noticed his gaze and blushed slightly, smiling quickly as if she didn't want him to know that she was unhappy.

'Maybe I will leave,' she said softly. 'Maybe it is time I did something different. But not with you. I'm not that stupid. My New Year's resolution is never to get involved with a man who is still in love with another woman and you fall into that category.'

Marco felt every muscle in his body tense but carefully controlled his facial expression. 'The only woman I love,' he purred softly, 'is currently parked outside this surgery with an engine problem. *She* is my baby.' He kept his tone neutral but Kate gave a faint smile and shook her head slowly.

'You don't fool me, Marco. Whenever Amy's name is mentioned, you always appear so cool and in control, but I know that you're not. What's happening under that cloak you put between yourself and the world?'

Nothing that he had any intention of sharing.

'You want to know what's under my cloak? This isn't the time or the place, *tesoro*.' How had they suddenly shifted from talking about her problems to talking about his? He teased her gently, swiftly and skilfully manoeuvring the con-versation back to safer ground. 'I have surgery starting in less than five minutes and that won't be enough to do justice to your beauty. When I make love to a woman, I need at least twenty-four hours.'

'Stop it or I'll have to throw a bucket of water over you!' Kate gave a reluctant laugh. 'It's bad enough that all the women in the village are in love with you. They're all waiting for your broken heart to heal so that they can pounce.'

'My heart isn't broken.' Marco reached forward and checked something on his computer. 'In fact, all my organs are intact and in perfect working order.'

'Well, don't tell anyone that! There'll be a stampede and we're busy enough here.' Kate's smile faded. 'I wish I was more like you. How do you do it? You and Amy were so in love—'

Taken aback by her frank, personal comment, Marco uttered a sharp expletive in Italian but then noticed the haunting sadness in Kate's eyes. With ruthless determination he pushed aside dark, swirling thoughts of his wife and focused his attention on his colleague. 'Kate…' With an effort, he kept his voice gentle. 'This is not about me, is it? It's about you. About you and Nick. Perhaps you should just tell him that you love him. Be honest.'

'What? I don't…' Flustered and embarrassed, Kate lifted a hand to her chest and shook her head in swift denial. 'What makes you say that? Marco, for goodness' sake…'

'Nick is the senior partner and my colleague,' Marco drawled softly, wondering why relationships were so incredibly complicated. 'You are also my colleague. It is hard to miss the tension between the two of you. Often I am in the middle of it.'

'Nick and I have known each other a long time.'

'*Sì*, I know that.' Marco sighed. 'You're in love with him. Tell him.'

'Even if you were right, which you're not,' Kate added quickly, her shoulders stiffening, 'you think I should just knock on the door of his consulting room and say, "I love you"?'

'Why not? It's the truth. Speaking as a man, I can tell you that we prefer a direct approach. Feminine games are an exhausting optional extra. If a woman wants to tell me that she loves me…' he shrugged expressively and lounged deeper in his chair '…why would I stop her?'

Kate laughed in disbelief. 'Sorry, but I'm just trying to picture Nick's face if I were to follow your advice.'

Marco watched her for a moment, noting the dark shadows under her eyes. 'Your problem is that you have fallen in love with an Englishman and English men know nothing about love. They are closed up, cold, unemotional. Give them twenty-four hours to make love to a woman and they would spend twenty-three of those hours watching football on the television.' As he'd planned, his words made her smile.

'Perhaps you're right.' She straightened her shoulders, suddenly looking less like a vulnerable woman and more like an efficient practice manager. 'You're a good friend. And for a man, you're very emotionally advanced. It would have been much simpler if I could have fallen for a hot Italian instead of a cold Englishman.'

Marco thought of his own disastrous marriage. 'Hot Italians can get it wrong, too,' he said wearily. *Badly wrong.* 'And Nick isn't really cold, just badly hurt. He carries a lot of guilt. A lot of pain. This has been a bad time in his life.'

A bad time in both their lives.

Given the events of the last few years, it was amazing that he and his partner were still managing to run a GP practice.

Reaching for his coffee, he cleared his mind of the dark thoughts that threatened to cloud the day.

Not now.

He wasn't going to think about that now.

It was the festive period and he had a punishing workload ahead of him.

There was going to be no time to brood or even think.

Which was exactly the way he wanted it.

* * *

Amy paused outside the surgery. The fresh sea air stung her cheeks and from above came the forlorn shriek of a seagull.

She had ten minutes before Marco was due to start seeing patients and she lost her chance to speak to him.

Ten minutes to finally end a marriage.

It would be more than enough time to say what had to be said. And he wouldn't be able to prolong the meeting because he would have patients waiting to see him.

Without giving herself time to change her mind, she pushed open the door and walked into Reception. The sudden warmth hit her and she walked up to the desk and saw Kate Althorp in conversation with the receptionist.

Once, they'd been friends even though the other woman was at least ten years her senior. Had that friendship ended with her sudden departure? Amy had no doubt that everyone in Penhally would have judged her harshly and she could hardly blame them for that. She'd given them no reason not to.

'Do you have an appointment?' Crisp, efficient and obviously busy despite the time of day, Kate glanced up and her eyes widened in recognition. '*Amy!* Oh, my goodness.' Abandoning her conversation, she walked round the desk towards Amy, clearly at a loss to know what to say. 'You're *home*? I thought you were still in Africa with that medical charity!'

'Not any more. Hello, Kate.'

Kate hesitated and then stepped forward and gave her a warm hug. 'It's good to see you, Amy. Really. Does Marco know you're here? Why didn't you call?'

'I was hoping— Marco doesn't know I'm here but I'd like to see him for a moment.' Amy cringed as she listened to herself. She hadn't seen her husband for two years and she was making it sound as though she'd just popped in to ask whether he'd be home in time for dinner.

Doubt flickered across Kate's face as she glanced in the

direction of the consulting rooms. 'He's about to start surgery and we've been incredibly busy because—'

'I know about Lucy and it's just for a moment,' Amy urged, unable to keep the note of desperation out of her voice. If Kate refused to let her see Marco that would mean waiting, and Amy wasn't sure that her courage would survive any sort of wait. She had to do this now. *Right now.* 'Please, Kate.' Unaccustomed to asking for help from another person, she stumbled over the words and the older woman looked at her for a moment, her responsibilities as practice manager clearly conflicting with her desire to help a friend so obviously in need.

After a moment of hesitation, Kate walked back round the desk and reached for the phone, her eyes still on Amy's face. 'I'll phone through to him and tell him that you're—'

'No!' Amy was already walking towards Marco's consulting room. 'I'll just go straight in.' Quickly, before she had time to change her mind.

Her heart pounding rhythmically against her chest, Amy tapped on his door.

'*Sì,* come in.'

The sound of his smooth, confident voice made her stomach lurch and she closed her eyes briefly. Despite his enviable fluency in English, no one could ever have mistaken Marco Avanti for anything other than an Italian and his voice stroked her nerve endings like a caress.

Her palm was damp with nerves as she clutched the doorhandle and turned it.

He was just a man like any other.

She wasn't going to go weak at the knees. She wasn't going to notice anything about him. She was past all that. She was just going to say what needed to be said and then leave.

Ten minutes, she reminded herself. She just had to survive ten minutes and not back down. And then she'd be on the train back to London.

She opened the door and stepped into the room. 'Hello, Marco.' Her heart fluttered like the wings of a captive butterfly as she forced herself to look at him. 'I wanted to have a quick word before you start surgery.'

His dark eyes met hers and heat erupted through her body, swift and deadly as a forest fire. From throat to pelvis she burned, her reaction to him as powerful as ever. Helplessly, she dug her fingers into her palms.

A man like any other? Had she really believed that, even for a moment? Marco was nothing like any other man.

She'd had two years to prepare herself for this moment, so why did the sight of him drive the last of her breath from her body? What was it about him? Yes, he was handsome but other men were handsome and she barely noticed them. Marco was different. Marco was the embodiment of everything it was to be male. He was strong, confident and unashamedly macho and no woman with a pulse could look at him and not want him.

And for a while he'd been hers.

She looked at him now, unable to think of anything but the hungry, all-consuming passion that had devoured them both.

His powerful body was ominously still, but he said nothing. He simply leaned slowly back in his chair and watched her in brooding silence, his long fingers toying with the pen that he'd been using when she'd entered the room.

Desperately unsettled, Amy sensed the slow simmer of emotion that lay beneath his neutral expression.

What wouldn't she have given to possess even a tiny fraction of his cool?

'We need to talk to each other.' She stayed in the doorway, her hands clasped nervously in front of her, a shiver passing through her body as the atmosphere in the room suddenly turned icy cold.

Finally he spoke. 'You have chosen an odd time of day for a reunion.'

'This isn't a reunion. We have things to discuss, you know we do.'

His gaze didn't flicker. 'And I have thirty sick patients to see before lunchtime. You shouldn't need to ask where my priorities lie.'

No, she didn't need to ask. His skill and dedication as a doctor was one of the qualities that had attracted her to him in the first place.

His handsome face was hard and unforgiving and she felt her insides sink with misery.

What had she expected?

He was hardly going to greet her warmly, was he? Not after the way she'd treated him. *Not after the things she'd let him think about her.* 'I didn't have any choice but to come and see you, Marco. You didn't answer my letters.'

'I didn't like the subject matter.' There was no missing the hard edge to his tone. 'Write about something that interests me and I'll consider replying. And now you need to leave because my first patient is waiting.'

'No.' Panic slid through her and she took a little step forward. 'We need to do this. I know you're upset, but—'

'Upset?' One dark eyebrow rose in sardonic appraisal. 'Why would you possibly think that?'

Her breathing was rapid. 'Please, don't play games—it isn't going to help either of us. Yes, I left, but it was the right thing to do, Marco. It was the right thing for both of us. I'm sure you can understand that now that some time has passed.'

'I understand that you walked out on our marriage. You think "upset"…' his accent thickened as he lingered on the word. 'You think "upset" is an accurate description of my feelings on this subject?'

Amy felt the colour touch her cheeks. The truth was that she had absolutely no insight into his feelings. She'd never really known what he had truly been feeling at any point in their relationship and she hadn't been around to witness his reaction to her departure. If he had been upset then she assumed that it would have been because she'd exposed him to the gossip of a small community, or possibly because he'd had a life plan and she'd ruined it. Not because he'd loved her, because she knew that had never been the case. How could he have loved her? What had she ever been able to offer a man like Marco Avanti?

Especially not once she'd discovered—

Unable to cope with that particular thought at the moment, Amy lifted her chin and ploughed on. 'I can see that you're angry and I don't blame you, but I didn't come here to argue. We can make this easy or we can make it difficult.'

'And I'm sure you're choosing easy.' The contempt in his tone stung like vinegar on an open wound. 'You chose to walk away rather than sort out a problem. Isn't that what you're good at?'

'Not every problem has a solution, Marco!' Frustrated and realising that if she wasn't careful she risked revealing more than she wanted to reveal, she moved closer to the desk. 'You have every right to be upset, but what we need now is to sort out the future. I just need you to agree to the divorce. Then you'll be free to...' *Marry another woman?* The words stuck in her throat.

'*Accidenti*, am I right in understanding that you have interrupted my morning surgery to *ask me for a divorce*?' He rose to his feet, his temper bubbling to the surface, a dangerous glint in his molten dark eyes. 'It is bad enough that I am expected to diagnose a multitude of potentially serious illnesses in a five-minute consultation, but now my wife decides that that in that same ridiculous time frame we are going to end our relationship. This is your idea of a joke, no?'

She'd forgotten how tall he was, how imposing. He topped six feet two and his shoulders were broad and powerful. Looking at him now, she had to force herself not to retreat to the safety of Reception. 'It's not a joke and if I'm interrupting your surgery, it's your fault. You wouldn't answer my letters. I had no other way of getting in touch with you. And this needn't take long.'

He gripped the edge of the desk and his knuckles whitened. 'Do you really think you can leave without explanation and then walk back in here and end our marriage with a five-minute conversation?' His eyes blazed with anger and his voice rose. *'Is that what you think?'*

Startled by his unexpected loss of control, Amy flinched. *She hadn't thought he'd cared so much.* Or was he angry because she'd chosen to confront him in his place of work? 'Don't shout—there are patients in Reception. They'll gossip.'

'Gossip? It's a little late to be worrying about gossip.' But he dropped back into his seat, threw her a dark, smouldering glance and then raked both hands through his glossy, dark hair. Several strands immediately flopped back over his forehead and she felt her breath catch.

The yearning to touch him was so powerful that she had to clasp her hands behind her back to prevent herself from reaching out and sliding her hands into his hair.

As if sensing her inner struggle, his gaze caught hers and held for a moment, his eyes darkening in a way that was achingly familiar. The atmosphere in the room shifted dangerously and awareness throbbed between them, drawing them into a tense, silent communication that said far more than words ever could.

Amy felt the instant response of her body. She felt her stomach quiver and her limbs warm.

It was still there, that inexplicable attraction that had

pulled them together with magnetic force from the moment they'd met.

Which meant that she had to get this over with. Quickly. Trying to ignore the insidious curl of feminine awareness deep in her pelvis, Amy gritted her teeth and backed towards the door.

This was why she'd gone so far away. She'd known that only by putting an ocean between them would she be able to resist the unbelievably powerful chemistry that knotted them together.

She had to leave.

Fast.

'Marco—it's all history, now. Let's not make this more painful than it has to be.'

'You're the one who made the whole thing painful, Amy.' His voice was suddenly dangerously quiet, but before he could say any more the door opened and Kate flew in.

'Marco, you have to see little Michelle right now! I've explained to your first patient that they're going to have to wait. I'm sorry.' She threw an apologetic look towards Amy. 'Is there any chance that you can grab a cup of coffee upstairs in the staffroom or something?'

Amy watched as Marco straightened his shoulders and wrenched back control. But his mind obviously wasn't on his work because for the briefest of moments his expression was blank. 'Michelle?' He said the name as if he'd never heard it before and Kate looked momentarily startled, as if detailed explanations were uncommon in their working relationship.

'Yes, Michelle! What's the matter with you?' Then she glanced at Amy and blushed slightly, as if she'd just realised what might be the matter. 'Michelle *Watson*. Carol said that she was off colour last night but she's suddenly gone downhill. She called an ambulance but they said that they'd be twenty minutes because they're stuck behind a gritting lorry. Honestly, Europe can have feet of snow and manage fine, but if we have so much as a dusting the entire country grinds to a halt. I'm tempted to go and organise them myself.'

'Michelle Watson. Of course. Michelle.' Marco uncoiled his lean, powerful body and rose to his feet again but there were lines of strain around his eyes. 'Bring her in.'

'Watson?' Amy remembered that Carol Watson had just delivered when she'd left and she glanced at Marco as Kate hurried out of the room. 'Carol's baby girl?'

'She isn't a baby any more.' His tone was flat and he didn't glance in her direction as if he was trying to get his mind firmly on the job. 'You've been gone two years and I don't have time to brief you on everything that has been happening in the village during your long absence.' He moved across the consulting room. 'You left, Amy. You made your choice.'

'Yes, but—' She broke off, wrestling against an instinctive desire to defend herself. What would he say if she told him the truth? Told him that she'd *had* to leave. *That she'd done it for him.* But she knew that she couldn't. She could never, ever tell him the truth because if he knew the truth then everything would become even more complicated. 'That's right.' She felt horrible. *Just horrible.* There was so much she wanted to say but she couldn't say any of it. 'I left.' Her voice shook but his swift glance was unsympathetic.

'Go and get a cup of coffee. Or just leave. It's what you're good at.'

'I can't leave until we've talked.'

He yanked open a cupboard and removed a pulse oximeter. 'Then you're going to have to wait until I have time to see you,' he growled. 'I think the current waiting time for an appointment with me is a week. Ask the girls at Reception. They just might be able to fit you in.'

CHAPTER TWO

THE door flew open and Kate hurried back into the room with Carol, who was carrying the toddler wrapped in a soft, pink blanket. A sulky-looking teenager followed them, her pretty face half hidden by a thick layer of make-up.

Amy was on the point of leaving the room and then she looked at the toddler and saw at a glance that Kate had been right to interrupt them. The child was fighting for each breath.

'Oh, Dr Avanti.' There was panic in Carol's voice. 'Thank goodness you're here. She's had this cold and I was up in the night with her and then this morning she just seemed so much worse. Her little chest was heaving so I panicked and called the ambulance but they're stuck on the coast road and you always know what to do so I just thought I'd come and take a chance in case—'

'*Calma.* Try and be calm, Carol.' Marco's voice was gentle and reassuring as his gaze rested on the child, his eyes sharp and observant. 'You did the right thing to come.'

Amy stepped forward, her own problems momentarily forgotten. 'Let me help. What do you want me to do, Marco?'

He glanced at her and then gave a brief nod. 'Let's give her some oxygen straight away.'

Amy located the oxygen and mask. 'Do you want me to set up a nebuliser?'

'To begin with I'll give her a beta 2 agonist via a spacer. It is better at this age than a nebuliser.' He turned back to the child and stroked his hand over the child's neck, palpating the neck muscles with gentle fingers. 'Michelle, what have you been doing, *angelo mia*? Are you worrying your poor mother?'

No one would have guessed that only moments earlier he'd been braced for a fight. All the hardness had gone from his tone and there was no trace of the anger that had been simmering inside him. Instead, he was kind and approachable, his smooth, confident movements removing the panic from the situation.

He'd always been amazing with children, Amy thought numbly as she handed him the oxygen mask. They found his strength reassuring and responded to his gentleness. *Strength and gentleness*. A killer combination. When she'd first met him he'd been working as a paediatrician and his skills in that field were very much in evidence as he assessed the little girl.

To someone who didn't know better it might have looked as though he was simply comforting the child and putting her at ease, but Amy watched the movement of his fingers and the direction of his gaze and knew that in that short space of time he'd checked the little girl's respirations, her pulse rate and the degree of wheezing.

Carol cuddled the child and looked at him helplessly. 'She ate a tiny bit of breakfast and then she was sick everywhere. After that she was just too breathless to eat. I've never seen her this bad.'

The teenager slumped against the wall and rolled her eyes. 'For goodness' sake Mum, stop panicking.' She broke off and coughed a few times. 'You make everything into such a drama.'

'Don't you tell me to stop panicking, Lizzie,' Carol snapped angrily. 'You were giving her breakfast! You should have noticed sooner that she wasn't breathing properly!'

'Well, I'm not a bloody doctor, am I?!' The tone was moody and defiant, but Amy saw the worry in the teenager's eyes and remembered that this was Carol's second marriage. Presumably Lizzie was her child from her previous marriage.

Clearly things weren't altogether harmonious in the household.

'She is here now and that is what is important.' Swiftly but calmly, Marco reached for the hand-held pulse oximeter, attached the probe to the child's finger. 'I want her as quiet as possible so that I can examine her properly. You will have a nice cuddle with your mama, Michelle. I'm going to help you with your breathing, *tesoro*.'

Tesoro.

Trying not to remember that he'd called her the same thing in happier times, Amy looked at the pulse oximeter.

'That's a neat device.' It was typical of Marco to have all the latest technology to hand, she mused silently. Oxygen, spacer, pulse oximeter. He may have chosen to move from paediatrics to general practice but he still insisted on having all the latest equipment.

'It's a very fast and reliable method of obtaining a reading.' He glanced at Carol, immediately offering an explanation. 'It tells me how much oxygen is in her blood. I'd like the level to be higher than it is. I'm going to give her something that will help her breathing.'

Carol's face was white and strained. 'Is it her asthma again?'

'*Sì*, it seems that way. She has had a virus and that can sometimes be a trigger.' He connected a face mask to the mouthpiece of a spacer.

'Michelle, I'm going to put this mask over your nose and mouth and I want you to just breathe normally.' He settled the mask gently over the child's face and actuated the inhaler. 'Just breathe for me now. Good girl. We'll start with this and see if this improves things.'

Michelle stared up at him in terror, her breath coming in rapid, rasping gasps.

Equally terrified, Carol rubbed her back gently. 'It's all right, darling. Dr Avanti is going to make you better. He always does, you know he does.'

The little girl clawed at her face, trying to remove the mask, and Marco gently took her hand and squatted down so that he was level with the child. 'Don't pull it off, *cucciola mia*.' His voice was deep and soothing. 'This mask is going to help you breathe and I want you to try and relax and forget it is there. You're going to listen to me instead of thinking of the mask. The mask is doing magic.' Still stroking the child's fingers with his own, he lifted his head and looked at Carol. 'What's her favourite story?'

'Story? I—I don't know…'

'"Sleeping Beauty",' Lizzie muttered, and Amy glanced towards her, surprised.

So she wasn't as indifferent as she seemed, then.

Assessing Michelle and sensing that Marco was going to choose to put a line in, Amy turned away and prepared an IV tray and then reached into the cupboard for hydrocortisone, which she was sure he was going to need.

'Ah, "Sleeping Beauty". That is my favourite, too.' Marco gave a smile that would have captivated the most cynical princess and stroked the little girl's blonde curls away from her face, his eyes flicking to her chest as he watched her breathing. 'So now I will tell you my version of the story. Once upon a time there was a beautiful princess called Michelle who lived in a wonderful castle by the sea— Amy?' His voice lowered. 'Can you get me a 24-gauge needle and fifty milligrams of hydrocortisone? Normally I would try oral medication but if she's vomiting, we'll go straight to IV.'

Their differences momentarily forgotten, Amy handed him the tray that she'd already prepared and he took it from her, still telling the story. 'Princess Michelle was very loved by her mummy and daddy and they decided to give her a big party for her birthday. Everyone was invited.' He was a natural storyteller, his Italian accent curling around the words as he calmed the child. She looked at him, clearly listening as he spoke, and Marco stroked the back of the little girl's hand, searching for a vein. Then he gave a nod and looked at Amy. 'Can you squeeze for me? Michelle, I'm just going to put a little tube into the back of your hand so that I can give you some extra medicine to make you feel better. More magic.'

Amy stared at Michelle's plump, tiny hand and was suddenly relieved that she wasn't the one searching for a vein.

Carol looked the other way, her teeth clamped on her lower lip. 'There isn't another doctor in the world I'd allow to do this,' she muttered, screwing up her face in trepidation. 'It's only because you used to be a kids' doctor and I know you've done it before. Her hands are so small, let alone her veins. I can't even think about it.'

Amy was inclined to agree.

She never could have chosen paediatrics as a speciality.

But Marco's expression didn't flicker and it was obvious that he wasn't concerned. This was where he excelled—where he was most comfortable. 'And Princess Michelle invited all her friends to her party and her big sister Princess Lizzie, who she loved very much.' He lifted his head briefly and flashed a smile at Lizzie, who blushed furiously under his warm, approving gaze.

'Michelle, you might feel a little scratch now.' The movement of his fingers was deliberate and confident as he slid the tiny needle through the child's skin and checked that he was in the vein. The child barely whimpered and Marco picked up the syringe of hydrocortisone, swiftly checked the ampoule and injected it into the child, barely pausing in his rendition of the story. 'And it was the biggest and the best party that anyone had ever been to. Everyone was in pretty dresses and there was dancing and Princess Lizzie met a handsome prince.'

'Not likely in boring old Penhally,' Lizzie muttered, and then started to cough again.

Marco dropped the empty syringe back onto the tray and lifted his gaze to the teenager. 'The prince was in disguise, passing through on his way home to his castle.' His eyes were amused and Amy watched as Lizzie gave a reluctant smile.

It was impossible not to respond to him, Amy thought helplessly. He charmed everyone, whatever their age. And he did it all while managing a potentially serious asthma attack.

Anyone who said that men were incapable of multi-tasking had never seen Marco dealing with an emergency. Perhaps that was one of the advantages of having spent so long in hospital medicine. Or perhaps he was just the sort of man who coped well under pressure.

Carol was still watching him anxiously. 'Will she have to go to hospital? My husband is waiting at the house to tell the ambulance where we are. Lizzie can run back and tell him what's going on.'

'Why me? Use the phone, Mum!' Lizzie's momentary good humour vanished and her tone was impatient. 'It's freezing out there!'

'Why can't you ever just *help*?' Clearly at the end of her tether, Carol snapped, and then pressed her lips together. 'All you ever think about is yourself!'

'Well someone has to because you obviously don't give a damn about me!'

Carol gasped. 'Elizabeth!!'

'Oh, get off my back!' Coughing again, Lizzie turned and

stamped out of the consulting room, slamming the door behind her.

Carol flinched, her face scarlet with embarrassment and anger. 'As if I haven't got enough on my plate,' she said in a shaky voice. 'I'm very sorry about that. I just don't know what's happening to Lizzie. She's undergone a complete personality change over the past few months. She used to be so sweet and loving. And she just adored Michelle. Now it's like living with a hand grenade.'

'She is a teenager,' Amy said quietly, aware that Marco was writing a letter to the hospital and needed to concentrate.

'She explodes at the slightest thing, she's out all hours and I never know where she is. She used to be top of her class and her marks have plummeted.' Carol cuddled Michelle closer. 'And she's been mixing with those awful Lovelace children and everyone knows what *they're* like. I see them on a Saturday night, just hanging around on the streets. I wouldn't be surprised if they're taking drugs…'

Reminded of the complexities of working in a community practice, Amy lifted a hand to her aching head and wondered how Marco managed to stay so relaxed.

He tapped a key on the computer and glanced at Carol. 'Have you spoken to the school about Lizzie?'

'Twice. They just gave me a standard lecture about handling teenage girls.'

The printer whirred into action. 'How bad are her mood swings?'

'Very.'

'I noticed she was coughing.' He took the letter from the printer and signed it. 'How long has she had that?'

'Coughing?' Carol looked a little startled. 'I don't know, really. A while, I think, now you mention it. Just an irritated sort of cough. I even asked her if she was smoking but she just gave me one of her looks and stomped out of the room.'

Marco put the letter in an envelope and handed it to her. 'Lizzie is reaching a difficult age, that's true,' he said softly. 'Not quite a woman but no longer a child. Unsure of who she is. A little rebellion is natural and good.'

'You think that's all it is?' The faith in Carol's eyes surprised Amy. It was quite obvious that the woman was ready to believe anything Marco told her.

'I think we should talk about it properly when there is more time.' He slipped his pen back into his pocket. 'For now your priority is Michelle. She has not improved as much as I would have liked so I want her to go to the hospital. In all probability she will be fine and we could monitor her here, but if we send her home, you will be worried.' He gave an expressive shrug that betrayed his Latin heritage. 'And you have already had enough worry for one day. So, we will send her to the hospital and then they can do the worrying. That will leave you free to give some attention to Lizzie.'

'I don't know what attention to give her,' Carol said flatly. 'It's like communicating with a firework. One minute she's inanimate, the next she's exploding in my face. I find it easier coping with toddlers than teenagers.'

Marco listened and then gave a lopsided smile. 'Being a mother is the hardest job in the world because your skills have to change all the time. You are a good mother and good mothers always find a way—remember that.'

Amy saw the gratitude on Carol's face and turned away for a moment, struggling with a painful lump in her throat. Why couldn't Marco have been careless and unfeeling? Even in a crisis he could see the bigger picture. He didn't just deal with the small child—he also handled the teenager and the worried mother.

She'd needed him to be unskilled and insensitive.

It would have made everything so much easier.

As it was, just ten minutes in his company had confirmed

SARAH MORGAN   33

her biggest dread. That two years of self-enforced absence
had made no difference to her feelings. She would love Marco
Avanti until she took her dying breath.

Marco picked up the phone and spoke to the paediatrician at
the hospital, keeping one eye on Michelle. He was concerned
that her breathing didn't seem to be improving as much as he
would have liked.

Had he missed something?

Was there something else he should have done?

He didn't usually have reason to question his medical skills
but neither was he usually expected to handle an emergency
while dealing with the unexpected appearance of his wife. Or
was she now an ex-wife? It was obvious that she considered
their relationship dead. And so had he. Until she'd walked into
the room and asked for a divorce.

Seriously unsettled for the first time in his adult life, he
ground his teeth, under no illusions that his concentration had
been severely tested by Amy's sudden and unannounced
arrival. Given that she clearly had no intention of leaving
until she'd said what she'd come to say, he needed to
somehow forget that she was there.

Forcing his mind back to Michelle, he ended the phone call
and then mentally ran through the algorithm for handling an
acute asthma attack in a toddler and assured himself that he'd
done everything that should be done.

The child needed to be in hospital. And his wife was
watching him, waiting for the right moment to ask him for a
divorce.

Why now? Why did she have to pick what must be the
busiest week of the year? And not only that, but they were a
doctor down. He didn't have the time to argue with her. Their
relationship was in its death throes and he didn't have the time
to try and save it.

Which had presumably been her intention. Why else would she have picked this particular moment out of all the moments that might have presented themselves over the past two years? Was she hoping that the pressures of work would make him easier on her?

Was she hoping that he'd just sign on the dotted line and sever all ties? Kill everything they'd ever shared?

The door opened and Kate bustled in. 'Carol, your husband redirected the ambulance and he's holding on right now on the phone. I have a paramedic in Reception, wanting to know if they're still needed. Are you planning to send Michelle to the hospital, Dr Avanti?'

Carol looked at Marco. 'You really think she should go in?'

Pushing aside his own problems, Marco gave a decisive nod. 'Definitely. I called the paediatrician and she's expecting Michelle. They'll admit her overnight, monitor her breathing and then assess her in the morning. We might need to change her medication. I'll speak to her once she's had a chance to examine Michelle.'

Carol closed her eyes briefly. 'It's so hard,' she whispered. 'She's so tiny and it's so, so scary. Worry, worry, worry, that's all I seem to do. I just want her to live a normal life and be like any other toddler. What's going to happen when she goes to school?'

'Carol, I know that you're worried but you have to take it one step at a time—isn't that the phrase you English use?' He placed a hand on her shoulder, his touch gentle. 'I will discuss her management with the hospital and you and I will watch her and see how she goes as winter progresses. And if, from time to time, she has a few problems then we will deal with those problems together. We are a team. If you have a worry, you make an appointment to see me and we sort it out. And soon we will find time to talk about your Lizzie.'

Carol's eyes filled and she bit her lip. 'Don't be kind because you'll make me cry.' She pressed a hand to her mouth. 'Sorry. You must think I'm such an idiot.'

'I think you're a loving mother who is tired and worried,' Marco said quietly, his gaze flicking to Michelle. An uneasy feeling stirred inside him. The little girl was pale and her respiratory rate was more rapid than he would have liked. Making a swift decision, he looked at Kate. 'I want to go in the ambulance with her.'

The practice manager didn't manage to hide her dismay. 'You're leaving in the middle of your surgery?'

Aware that Carol was listening, Marco tried humour. 'Not in the middle,' he drawled, reaching for his bag. 'I haven't actually started yet.'

Kate shook her head, despair in her voice. 'Marco, we have patients queuing halfway back to the next county. Dr Tremayne and Dr Lovak are already seeing patients and with Lucy gone—'

'We have a sick child here who needs my care,' Marco reminded her softly, dropping a bronchodilator into his bag.

Kate gave him a desperate look and then sighed. 'Of course. Go with Michelle. That has to be the priority. We'll manage here. Somehow.'

Carol glanced between them, her expression guilty. 'I'm *really* sorry.'

'You have no reason to be sorry,' Marco said swiftly. 'In this practice each patient gets the attention they need when they most need it. The patients will not mind because they know that next time it could be them.'

Judging from the expression on Kate's face she wasn't convinced and Marco thought for a moment, aware that he was leaving her and the receptionists to cope alone with the flak from the patients. His gaze settled on Amy, who stood in the corner of his consulting room, looking awkward and out of place. 'Amy can take the rest of my surgery. That will save Nick and Dragan having to see extra patients.'

Judging from her shocked expression he might as well have suggested that she run naked along the harbour wall.

'I— *Me*?'

'Yes, you. You're a qualified GP.' He added a few more bits to his bag. 'You happen to have arrived when we're in crisis. I'm sure you won't mind helping out.'

'But—'

'What a brilliant idea! That would be fantastic,' Kate enthused, her relief evident as she ushered Carol towards the door, catching the pink blanket before it slid to the floor. 'I'll help Carol and Michelle into the ambulance while you pack what you need, Marco. Join us when you're ready. Then I'll come back and brief you, Amy. You can use Lucy's consulting room.'

Amy's expression was close to panic. 'But I'm not staying—' The door closed behind Kate and Amy flinched and turned to Marco, her hands spread in a silent plea. 'Marco, this is ridiculous. I just need to talk to you for five minutes, that's all.'

'As you can clearly see, I don't have five minutes. I don't have one minute. I can't talk to you until the patients have been seen.' Strengthened by the prospect of a brief respite before the inevitable confrontation, Marco snapped his bag shut with a force that threatened the lock. 'If you want to talk to me, help with surgery. Then perhaps I'll find time to talk to you.'

'But—'

He lifted the bag. 'That's my price for a conversation.'

'We *have* to talk, you know we do.' She wrapped her arms around her waist and then let them drop to her sides and gave a sigh. 'You don't leave me with much choice.'

'About as much choice as you gave me when you walked

away from our relationship.' He glanced out of the window, remembered the snow and reached for his coat. Suddenly he couldn't wait to put distance between them. He was angry with her. *And angry with himself for still caring so much after two years.* He needed space. Needed perspective. He needed to work out what he was going to do. 'It's non-negotiable, Amy. If you want to talk to me, stay and do the surgery. When the patients have been seen, I might find time to listen to you.'

'If you can't find anything, just let me know.' Kate threw open a few more cupboards and waved a hand vaguely. 'Everything you're likely to need should be here. And if you need any inside information on the patients, Nick should be able to help. Press 2 on your phone and you're straight through to him.'

Nick Tremayne, the senior partner. Although he was a good friend of Marco's, Amy had always found him more than a little intimidating.

What would he think of her being there? Just after she'd left Marco, Nick himself had suffered tragedy when his wife, Annabel, had died suddenly.

'How is Nick? I was so shocked when I received your letter telling me the news.'

'Yes.' Kate slipped a pile of blank prescriptions into the printer, her face expressionless. 'We were all shocked. I thought you ought to know, although finding an address for you was a nightmare. Even the medical charity you were working for didn't seem able to guarantee that they could get it to you.'

'I was moving around. It took about six months to catch up with me.' Amy sank into the chair, remembering how awful she'd felt when she'd read the news. 'I wrote to him. Just a card. Is he—is he doing all right?'

Kate reached for a pen from the holder on the desk. 'I suppose so. He just carries on. Doesn't give much away. Lucy's baby will help, I suppose. They've called her Annabel.'

'Oh, that's lovely,' Amy said softly. 'I bumped into Tony earlier. He said the baby was premature?'

'Yes, she was born a few weeks early but she's doing fine by all accounts. Still in Special Care but once they're happy with her feeding, she should be home.'

'And Nick—has he met anyone else?'

The pen that Kate was holding slipped to the floor. 'He dates plenty of people.' She stooped and picked up the pen, her voice slightly muffled. 'But I don't think any of them are serious. Are you ready? I'll send in your first patient.'

Amy slid a hand over the desk and looked at the computer, feeling as though she was on a runaway train. She'd come to talk to Marco and here she was sitting in a consulting room, preparing to take a surgery. What had happened to her ability to say no? 'How many patients?'

'You don't want to know but let's just say that Marco is a very, very popular doctor around here. If Dragan Lovak gets any cancellations, I'll send a few his way.' Kate smiled. 'This is so kind of you, Amy. We really appreciate it. I've been trying unsuccessfully to find locum cover for the past few weeks but no one wants to spend Christmas and New Year in freezing Cornwall at short notice. You're a lifesaver.'

A lifesaver? Amy bit back a hysterical laugh. She didn't feel like a lifesaver. She felt like the one who was drowning. 'I'm not sure how much use I'll be. I won't know any of the patients.' She felt a brief flutter of anxiety. During her time in Africa, her focus had been on tropical diseases. Was she capable of running a busy surgery?

'You're a qualified doctor. That makes you of use.' Kate leaned across and flicked on the computer on her desk. 'Hit this key to get everything up on the computer. You'll be fine.

You've been working in deepest Africa for the past two years so the problems of a little Cornish town should seem like a walk in the park by comparison.'

Suddenly she craved Africa. *Craved distance from Marco.* Amy closed her eyes briefly and tried not to think about what was going to happen when he returned. It was clear that there was no way the conversation was going to be easy. 'Kate, how do I call the patients?'

'There's a buzzer right there.' Kate moved a pile of papers. 'List of hospital consultants in your top drawer, just in case you need to refer anyone.'

Amy watched her go and then reached out and pressed the buzzer before she could change her mind. She squashed down a flicker of anxiety and smiled as her first patient was walking into the room.

'Hello, Mrs…' Amy checked the screen quickly '…Duncan. Dr Avanti has had an emergency trip to the hospital with a child so I'm covering his surgery. How can I help you?'

'I've been feeling rotten for a couple of days. Since Christmas Day, I suppose.' Paula Duncan sank onto the chair and let her handbag slip to the floor. 'I assumed it was the flu or something—there's so much of it around. I wasn't even going to bother making an appointment but this morning my head started hurting and I've had this numbness and tingling around my right eye.'

Amy stood up, her attention caught. 'How long have you had that rash on your nose?'

'I woke up with it. Lovely, isn't it?' Mrs Duncan lifted a hand to her face and gave a weary laugh. 'On top of everything else, I have to look like a clown. I can throw away the dress I bought for the New Year's Eve party, that's for sure. Unless the Penhally Arms decide to turn it into a masked ball.'

Amy examined the rash carefully and remembered seeing

a patient with a similar rash in one of her clinics in Africa. 'It started this morning?'

'Yes. Just when you think life can't get any worse, it gets worse.'

Thinking of her own situation, Amy gave a faint smile. 'I know what you mean.'

'If I wasn't in so much pain I'd be really embarrassed to be seen out but I don't even care any more. I just hope there's something you can do. I have no idea where the rash has come from. I spent Christmas on my own so I can't imagine that I've caught anything.'

Amy washed her hands and sat back down at her desk. 'The rash suggests to me that you have ophthalmic shingles, Mrs Duncan. I'm going to send you up to the hospital to see the ophthalmologist—an eye doctor.'

'Shingles?' The woman stared at her. 'That's like chickenpox, isn't it? And in my eye? Surely that isn't possible.'

'I'm afraid it's entirely possible.' Amy opened the drawer and pulled out the list of consultants that Kate had mentioned. She'd had no idea that she'd be using it so soon. 'It's caused by the same virus.'

'So I *must* have been in contact with someone with chickenpox? But who? I don't even know any small children!'

Amy shook her head. 'It doesn't work like that. There's no evidence that you can catch shingles from chickenpox, although it can occasionally happen the other way round if a person isn't immune. But once you've had chickenpox, the virus lies dormant and then flares up again at some point.'

'Can we let it go on its own? Why do I need to see an eye doctor?'

'The rash on your nose means that it's likely that your eye is affected. The ophthalmologist will give you a full examination and follow-up. But I'm going to give you a prescription that I want you to take.'

'Drugs?'

'Yes. Aciclovir.' Amy selected the drug she wanted on the computer screen and the printer next to her purred softly. 'I don't always prescribe it, but if it's within seventy-two hours of the symptoms starting then there's a good chance that it can lower the risk of you developing post-herpatic pain. Hopefully, in your case, it will help. Take it with you to the consultant in case he wants to give you something different.'

Mrs Duncan tucked the prescription into her bag. 'So I have to go there now?'

'Go straight to the eye ward. I'll call them so that they're expecting you.'

Mrs Duncan rose to her feet. 'Thank you.' She looked stunned. 'I don't know what I was expecting but it wasn't that.'

'If you have any questions you can always come back and talk to me.'

And then Amy realised that she wasn't going to be here. In a few hours she'd be gone. She glanced at her watch and wondered how long Marco was going to be. Was Michelle all right? It felt strange to be back in England, taking a surgery.

She saw a seemingly endless stream of patients and then Nick Tremayne walked into the room.

'Nick.' Flustered, Amy rose to her feet. 'I— It's good to see you.'

'It's good to see you, too.' His gaze was quizzical. 'And surprising.'

'Yes. I— Marco and I had things to talk about and then things became very busy and so I said I'd help out.' She sank back into her chair and he gave a faint smile.

'We're glad you're helping out. How are you?'

'Good,' she lied. 'And you? I hear that Lucy's made you a grandfather! Congratulations. Although I must say you look far too young to be anyone's grandfather.'

'That's what happens when you have your own children young,' Nick said drily. 'So how was Africa?'

'Interesting.' *Miserable.* She hesitated, unsure what to say but knowing that she had to say something about the sudden death of his wife. 'I was so sorry to hear about Annabel, Nick.'

'I was grateful for your card.' He was cool and matter-of-fact, revealing nothing of his emotions. 'So what are your plans, Amy?'

Divorce. 'I'm not sure, yet. Marco and I need to talk.'

Nick nodded. 'Well, if you have any problems with the rest of his surgery, just call through to me or Dragan.'

'Thanks.' Amy watched him leave and moments later Kate appeared with a cup of coffee. 'Is that for me?'

'You've earned it. I can see the floor in the waiting room now, so that's a good sign.'

'Is Marco back?'

'Yes, but he had to go straight out again. Man from the brewery developed chest pains while he was making a delivery at the Penhally Arms. Probably the weight of the alcohol we're all going to drink on New Year's Eve.' Kate put the coffee on the desk. 'Black, no sugar. Is that right?'

Amy glanced at her in surprise. 'Yes. Thank you.'

'Tip from Marco. He said that you're useless in the morning unless you've had your coffee.'

Memories of long, lazy mornings lounging in bed with Marco filled her brain and Amy felt the colour flood into her cheeks. She reached out a hand and buzzed for the next patient. 'Right, well, thanks, Kate. I suppose I'd better get on. Is it always like this?'

Kate laughed. 'No, sometimes it's busy.'

Thinking of the number of patients she'd seen so far, Amy suddenly realised that Marco probably hadn't been playing games when he'd said he didn't have time for conversation.

'Dr Avanti?' A man hesitated in the doorway and Amy smiled, recognising him immediately. *A face from her childhood.*

'Rob! How are you?' She blushed and waved an apologetic hand. 'Sorry. Obviously you're not that great or you wouldn't be spending your morning in the doctor's surgery. How can I help you?' It felt weird, sitting here, talking to someone that she'd known as a child. Rob, a trawlerman, was part of her childhood. How many hours had she spent watching him bring in the boat and haul in the catch?

And how did he see her? As someone who was still a child?

Or as someone who was capable of handling his medical problems?

'My hand is agony.' Without hesitation, he sat down and took off his coat. 'Been like this for a few days. I thought it might settle but it's getting worse and the rash is going up my arm.'

Amy leaned forward and took a closer look at his hand, noticing the inflammation and the discolouration spreading up his arm. Her mind went blank and she knew a moment of panic. *What was it?* 'Have you been bitten? Scratched?' She lifted his hand, noticing that Rob flinched at her touch. 'That's tender?'

'Very.' He frowned thoughtfully down at his hand. 'I don't think I've scratched myself but you know what it's like, handling fish. It's pretty easy to get a cut from a fish spine or the bones. Then there's the broken ends of warps—to be honest, we're too busy to be checking for minor injuries all the time. Aches and pains and cuts are all just part of the job.'

Fish. Of course. Amy studied his hand again, noticing the raised purple margin around the reddened area and the pus. *Erysipeloid.* For a moment she forgot Marco and the real reason that she was sitting in the surgery. She forgot all her own problems in her fascination of practising medicine. 'I think that's probably what has happened, Rob. You must have scratched yourself without knowing and that's allowed an infection to get hold. Bacteria are easily carried into the wound from fish slime and guts.' She ran her fingers gently over his arm, taking a closer look. 'I'll give you some antibiotics. Are you allergic to penicillin?'

'Not to my knowledge. So you've seen this before, then?'

'Actually, no, but I've read about it.' Amy turned back to the computer, hit a few keys and then scrolled down to find the drug she wanted. 'Fishermen are particularly prone to infections of the hands and fingers because of the work they do. This particular infection is called erysipeloid. I'll give you an antibiotic and that should do the trick, but prevention is better than cure, Rob. You should be spraying disinfectant over the surfaces where you work and using a hand wash after handling fish. Something like chlorhexidine gluconate would do the trick.'

Rob pulled down his sleeve. 'It's there, but we don't always use it. When you're hauling in nets and fighting the wind and the waves, it doesn't seem like a high priority.'

Amy signed the prescription. 'Take these, but if it gets worse, come back.'

Rob stood up, his eyes curious. 'Little Amy. I remember you when you were knee high.' His voice gruff, he slipped the prescription into his pocket. 'Every summer you visited your grandmother and stayed in that tiny cottage by the shore. Always on your own, you were. You never joined in with any of the local kids. You used to stand on the harbour wall and watch us bring in the catch. You were all solemn-eyed and serious, as if you were wondering whether to run away to sea.'

Amy stared at him, unable to breathe.

She *had* been wondering whether to run away to sea. Every morning she'd scurried down to the harbour and watched the boats sail away, all the time wishing that she could go with the tide and find an entirely new life. A better life.

Happiness doesn't just land in your lap, Amy, you have to chase it.

Rob frowned. 'You all right? You're a bit white.'

Tripped up by the memories of her grandmother, Amy somehow managed to smile. 'That's right. I loved staying here.'

'She was a good woman, your grandmother. And she was so proud of you.'

Feeling her poise and professionalism unravel like a ball of wool in the paws of a kitten, Amy swallowed. 'She always wanted me to be a doctor.'

'And didn't we know it.' Rob grinned. 'Couldn't walk past her in the village without hearing the latest story about her clever granddaughter.' His smile became nostalgic. 'She's missed is Eleanor. But that young couple you sold the cottage to are very happy. The Dodds. They've got two children now.'

'Good.' Desperate to end the conversation, Amy rose to her feet and walked towards the door. 'Come back to one of the doctors if you have problems with your hand, Rob.'

He didn't move, as if he sensed some of the turmoil inside her. 'She wanted to see you married with children—would have loved to see you together, you and Dr Avanti. It's good that you're back. And it's great for the practice. I know how much they're struggling with Lucy going into labour so suddenly.'

Back? 'I'm not exactly— I mean, that isn't why—' She broke off and gave a weak smile. 'It's lovely to see you, Rob.' There was no point in explaining that she wasn't staying—that she should already have been back at the train station. They'd find out soon enough that her visit had been fleeting and she wouldn't need to give explanations because she wouldn't be here.

Feeling a twinge of guilt that she was going to be leaving Marco to deal with still more gossip, Amy showed Rob out of the consulting room and then returned to her desk and sank onto her chair with her head in her hands, the lump building in her throat as memories swirled around her exhausted mind.

'So—judging from the expression on your face, delivering patient care in Penhally isn't any easier than it was in Africa.' Marco's smooth, accented tones cut through her misery and she jumped and let her hands fall into her lap.

Even though she'd been longing to have the conversation with him, now the moment had arrived she wasn't entirely sure she could cope with it.

CHAPTER THREE

'Marco. I—I didn't hear you come in.'

'Presumably because you were miles away.' He pushed the door shut with the flat of his hand and strolled into the room, his cool control in direct contrast to her own nervous agitation. 'You look pale. What's the matter?'

That was twice in five minutes she'd been told that she looked pale. Making a mental note to dig out a pot of blusher and use it, Amy gave a humourless laugh. 'I would have thought it was obvious.'

'Not to me. Any woman who finds it that easy to walk away from a marriage can't possibly be daunted by the prospect of spending a few hours wandering down memory lane.'

He had no idea.

And that was her fault, of course, because she hadn't wanted him to know the truth. She'd wanted to spare him a difficult decision. Wanted to spare them both the slow, inevitable destruction of their marriage. So she'd made the decision for both of them and gone for a quick, sudden end. She'd thought it would make it less painful in the long term.

Now she wasn't so sure. *Could the pain have been worse?*

'It wasn't easy for me, Marco.' She didn't want him thinking that and she looked at him, almost hating him for his insensitivity but at the same time relieved, because she knew that his anger made him blind. Anger would prevent him from delving deeper into her reasons for leaving. *And she didn't want him delving.* 'I did what was right for both of us.'

'No, you did what was right for you. I wasn't involved in the decision.' He prowled across the consulting room to the desk where she was seated. 'One minute we were planning a future, the next you decided that you were going to spend the future on your own. There was no discussion. You gave me no choice.'

In a way, that was true, and yet she knew that the decision she'd made had been the right one.

'Do you want to talk about this now?' Strangely enough, even though she was the one who'd pushed, she just didn't feel prepared to say what had to be said. In Africa she'd thought she'd resigned herself to the reality of her life, but one look at Marco had unravelled her resolve.

'That was the reason you came, wasn't it?'

Feeling vulnerable next to his superior height, she rose to her feet and their eyes locked. 'All right, let's have this discussion and then we can both get on with our lives. I ended our marriage, yes, that's true.'

'You left without talking it through with me.'

'I *did* talk to you!'

'When?'

'I told you I was unhappy. We should never have moved back to Penhally. It was a mistake.' She sank back into her chair because her legs just wouldn't hold her any longer. 'I didn't feel the way I thought I was going to feel.'

'You underwent a complete personality transformation!' Anger shimmered in his eyes. 'One moment you were lying in my bed, planning our future, and the next thing you were packing your bag so quickly you almost bruised yourself running through the front door. It didn't make sense.'

It would have made perfect sense if he'd known what she'd discovered.

'I didn't have a personality transformation,' she said stiffly. 'I just changed my mind about what I wanted. People do it every day of their lives and it's sad, but it's just one of those things. The reason you're angry is because you felt that you weren't part of the decision and you always have to be in control.'

'Control?' He lifted an eyebrow in cool appraisal. 'You saw our relationship as a power struggle, *amore*?'

Unsettled by the look in his eyes and the sheer impact of his physical presence, she left her chair and walked to the window, keeping her back to him. 'It's time to be honest about this. We made a mistake, Marco. We never should have married. I mean, it was all far, far too quick! Three months! Three months is nothing!' She fixed her gaze on a point in the distance and recited the words she'd rehearsed so many times. 'How can anyone know each other in three months? Yes, there was chemistry, I'm not denying that. But chemistry alone isn't enough to bind a couple together for a lifetime.'

There was an ominous silence and when he finally spoke his voice was clipped. 'You're describing hormonal teenagers. We were both adults and we knew what we wanted.'

'Adult or not, the chemistry was still there. The relationship was fine, but marriage—that was a stupid impulse.' *A fleeting dream that had been cruelly snatched away.* She could feel his gaze burning a hole between her shoulder blades and this time it took him almost a full minute to reply.

'At least have the courtesy to look at me when you reduce our relationship to nothing but a sordid affair.' There was a dangerous note in his voice and she took a deep breath and turned slowly, struggling to display the calm and neutrality that she knew she needed in order to be convincing.

'Not sordid, Marco,' she said quietly, hoping that her voice was going to hold out. 'It was amazing, we both know that. But it was never going to last. We shouldn't have tried to hold onto it or make it into something that it wasn't. We wanted different things.'

He watched her for a moment, his eyes intent on her face as if her mind were a book and he were leafing through every single page, searching for clues. 'Until we returned to Penhally, I wasn't aware that we wanted different things. We'd made plans for the future. I was going to work with Nick in the practice and you were going to stay at home and have our babies until you decided to return to work. It was the reason we chose the house.'

She inhaled sharply, unable to stifle the reaction. *She couldn't even bear to think about the house.* 'I'm sorry I didn't keep my end of the bargain. I'm sorry I decided that I wanted a career instead of a family.'

He looked at her as if she were a complete stranger and then he muttered something in Italian that she didn't understand and Amy looked at him helplessly.

'If this conversation is going to have any hope of working then you at least have to speak English so that I can understand you.'

'*You* are speaking English and I don't understand you at all! The complexities of this situation appear to transcend the language barrier.' He raked long bronzed fingers through his glossy dark hair. 'You talk about wanting a career, and yet when we first met you talked about nothing but family and children. You were soft, gentle, giving. Then we moved to Penhally and suddenly, whoosh...' He waved a hand expressively. 'You underwent this transformation. Soft, affectionate Amy became hard, distant Amy. And distant Amy suddenly became career Amy. It was as if the woman I was with suddenly reinvented herself. What happened? *What happened to change everything?*'

She stared at him blankly, teetering on the edge of confession. It would have been so easy. So easy to tell him exactly what had happened.

But that would have made things so much more complicated and they were already more complicated than she could comfortably handle.

The truth created a bad taste in her mouth and for a moment she just stood there, trapped by the secrets and lies that she'd used to protect him. 'I suppose it was several things.' With an effort, she kept her tone careless. 'Penhally isn't exactly the centre of the universe. There wasn't enough to keep me occupied. I was bored. I missed medicine. I missed the patients.' It was true, she consoled herself, she *had* missed the patients.

'If that was the case, you should have said so and we could have found you work, if not in Penhally then at another surgery.' Marco turned and paced across the surgery, as if he found the confined space intolerable.

'It's all history now,' Amy murmured. 'Going over it again is going to achieve nothing. It's time to move on, Marco. Let's just have the discussion that we need to have and then I'll leave you in peace.'

'Peace?' He turned, his eyes glinting dangerously, his lean, handsome face taut. 'Is that what you think leaving will give me when you walk out again? Peace? I haven't known a moment's peace since you left.'

He hadn't?

Her heart gave a little lift and then crashed down again as she realised that his feelings made absolutely no difference to what she had to do. And anyway his feelings had more to do with injured pride and inconvenience than anything deeper. Marco Avanti was a man who knew what he wanted out of life and she'd temporarily derailed his plans—that was all.

'I'm sorry,' she said softly, telling the truth for the first time since she'd walked into Penhally. 'Truly I'm sorry for any hurt I've caused.'

He watched her, his eyes sharp on her face. 'But you're still asking me for a divorce?'

For the space of a heartbeat she paused. 'Yes,' she croaked. 'I am. It's the only course of action.'

'*Not* the only course.' He strolled towards her and then stopped. 'I never thought of you as a quitter, Amy, and yet you haven't once mentioned trying again. Instead of abandoning our marriage, you could try and fix it.'

She froze as he dangled temptation in front of her and her heart stumbled in her chest. Like an addict she gazed at him and then she remembered how far she'd come, how much she'd already suffered to get to this point, and shook her head. 'It isn't fixable.'

'You don't know that because you haven't tried. And this time we'd be trying together. Talk to me, Amy, and we can fix it.'

'You can't fix something when the two halves don't match. We want different things. You want a family, Marco. You made that clear on many occasions. Women have been chasing you for years, but you never settled down with any of them because you weren't ready to have children. But then suddenly that changed.'

'It changed when I met you. The first thing I thought when I laid eyes on you was that you were the sexiest woman I'd ever seen.' His voice was a soft, seductive purr. 'You were wearing that little navy suit with a pair of high heels and your legs came close to being the eighth wonder of the world. You were serious and studious and didn't stop asking me questions.'

She felt the colour rush into her cheeks. 'You just happened to be lecturing on an aspect of paediatrics that interested me.'

'Then, when I stopped looking at your legs and your beautiful brown eyes, I realised how intelligent you were and how warm and kind. I knew immediately that you were the woman I wanted to be the mother of my children. I knew it in a moment.'

The mother of his children.

There was a long, tortured silence. Knowing that some response was required, Amy tried to speak but her voice just refused to work. Instead, she stooped, picked up her bag and yanked her coat from the back of the chair. Only once she'd slipped her arms into the sleeves and belted the waist did she find her voice.

'I'm sorry I ruined your plans, but I can't be the mother of your children, so it's time you started searching for another candidate. And now I have to go.' *Before she collapsed in front of him.*

'I thought you wanted to talk to me?'

'It's not— I can't...' Needing fresh air and space, she stumbled over the words. 'You're just too busy. I shouldn't have come, I see that now. I'll leave you to see your patients and I'll write to you again and perhaps this time you'll reply. It's the best thing for both of us.' She moved towards the door but he caught her arm, his strong fingers biting through the wool of her coat as he pulled her inexorably towards him.

'You came all this way to talk.' He held her firmly. 'And we haven't finished. Last time you just walked out and you wouldn't listen to me. You're not doing that again, Amy.'

Why had she ever thought that seeing him face to face was a good idea?

'You still have patients waiting.'

'I'll see my patients. Then I'll buy you lunch at the Smugglers' Inn. We can talk then.'

He couldn't have picked a place more public. 'You want to be the subject of gossip?'

'Gossip doesn't worry me and never will. Kate will make

you a cup of coffee and find you somewhere to sit. Then I'll give you a lift.'

She gave a faint smile. 'The Maserati has learned to cope with snow?'

'She is moody and unpredictable, that's true, but it is just a question of handling her correctly.' His eyes held hers and she wondered briefly whether he was talking about the car or her.

'You don't need to give me a lift. I'll wander around the village for an hour or so and then meet you up there. The walk up the coast road will do me good. But I'm going back to London tonight.'

His eyes narrowed slightly and his expression was unreadable. 'So that means that you have plenty of time for lunch. Twelve-thirty. Be there or this time I'll come looking for you.'

The Smugglers' Inn was perched near the edge of the cliff on the coast road, a short drive out of Penhally.

The Maserati gave a throaty growl as Marco turned into the car park. He turned off the engine and sat for a moment, breathing in the scent of leather. Usually the car calmed him but today he felt nothing, his body too tense after his encounter with Amy.

With a soft curse he locked the car and walked towards the pub, distracted for a moment by the wild crash of the waves on the rocks below. The temperature had dropped and Marco stood for a moment, trying to formulate a plan, but his normally sharp brain refused to co-operate and he suddenly realised that he had no idea what he was going to do or say.

The irony of the situation didn't escape him. Of all the women who'd wanted to settle down with him over the years, he'd finally picked one who was wedded to her career and wasn't interested in having children.

He frowned. Except that she *had* been interested in having children. More than interested. At the time, he'd assumed that her longing for a family stemmed from the disappointing relationship that she'd apparently had with her own mother. Perhaps he'd been wrong about that. Perhaps he'd been wrong about all of it.

It was true that people changed their minds, but still…

He should give her a divorce, he told himself grimly, because that was clearly what she wanted and, anyway, she'd been gone for two years. What was there to salvage?

Anger exploded inside him once again and he took a deep breath of cold, calming air before turning towards the pub. With only a slight hesitation he pushed open the heavy door and walked inside.

Warmth, laughter and the steady buzz of conversation wrapped itself around him and drew him in. Immediately his eyes scanned the bar, searching for Amy.

Would she be there or had she run? Was she now shivering on the station platform, waiting for the train that would take her away from him?

How badly did she want the divorce?

And then he saw her, a slight figure, huddled on her own by the blazing fire, still wearing her coat and scarf as if all the heat in the world wouldn't warm her. She looked out of place and vulnerable. Her dark hair had been smoothed behind one ear and Marco felt something stir inside him as he remembered all the times he'd kissed her slender neck, *the tempting hollow of her throat…*

He dragged his eyes from her neckline, frustrated by the unexpectedly powerful surge of lust that gripped him.

So, people were wrong about some things, he thought bitterly. *Time didn't always heal.* In his case, time hadn't healed at all. Despite everything, Amy still affected him more than any woman he'd ever met.

His jaw clenched and he stood for a moment, feeling the now familiar tension knot inside him. Why? Was it because she was the only woman who had walked away from him? Was this all about his ego?

Was he really that shallow?

And then the lust was replaced by anger and he didn't even try and subdue it because over the past two years he'd learned that anger was the easiest emotion to deal with. Anger was so much better than pain and disillusionment.

Back in control, he strolled across the room and nodded to the man behind the bar. 'Tony. Give me something long and cold that isn't going to dull my senses.'

The landlord's gaze flickered towards Amy, who was still staring blankly into the fire. 'Looks to me as though you might need something stronger.'

'Don't tempt me. I've always found that my diagnostic abilities are better when I'm sober, and I'm on call. Has she ordered?' No point in pretending that his ex-wife hadn't just appeared out of nowhere with no warning. The locals had eyes and he had no doubt that they'd be using them.

Tony reached for a glass and snapped the cap off a couple of bottles. 'Arrived ten minutes ago. Paid for a grapefruit juice, made polite conversation for about three seconds and then slunk into the corner like a wounded animal. Hasn't touched her drink. If you want my opinion, she's not a happy woman. You might want to use your famous doctoring skills to find out what's bothering her.'

Marco's long fingers drummed a steady rhythm on the bar. *He knew exactly what was bothering her.* She wanted a quick and easy divorce and he wasn't playing ball.

The landlord poured the contents of the bottles into the glass. 'Here you go. One doctor-on-duty fruit cocktail. Full of vitamins, totally devoid of alcohol. No charge. If you want to eat, let me know. Cornish pasties came out of the oven five minutes ago and the fish and chips are good, but I'm guessing you don't want to feast on cholesterol in front of your patients.'

Marco gave a faint smile, took the drink and strolled across to the fire. 'Sorry I've kept you waiting.' He put his glass down on the table and shrugged off his coat. 'Our patients haven't quite got the hang of developing ailments that can be seen easily within the allotted time.'

'It doesn't matter.' She looked across at him, the flickering fire sending red lights through her dark hair. Away from the pressure of the surgery he noticed that her face was paler than ever and there were dark shadows under her eyes. And she'd definitely lost weight since he'd last seen her.

He studied her thoughtfully.

For a woman following her chosen path of career over motherhood, she didn't appear either settled or happy.

Was something wrong with her? Something other than the prospect of a divorce? Had she picked up some tropical disease while she'd been working in Africa?

'So...' he lifted his drink '...tell me about your work. Is it hard?' Was that why she was so pale? Did her work explain the weight loss? Had she been ill?

'Sorry?' She glanced at him, her expression blank, as if she hadn't heard him.

'Your work. The thing you care most about, remember, *tesoro*?' It was hard not to keep the irony out of his voice. 'How is this amazing career that was so much more important to you than marriage and children?'

'My career?' She gave a little start, as though she'd forgotten that she even had a career. Then she straightened her shoulders, her gaze returning to the fire. 'Yes. I was running a malaria project.'

'And that was interesting? Fulfilling?' *Why wouldn't she look at him?*

'Yes.'

Marco felt the anger surge again and struggled against the temptation to slide his hand around the back of her neck and force her to meet his gaze. 'Worth sacrificing our marriage for?'

Her breathing quickened and her eyes slid to his. 'Our marriage was something separate.'

'No.' He growled the word and noticed a few heads turn towards them. *Why had he decided to have this discussion in a pub?* 'It wasn't separate, Amy. You ended our marriage because you chose a career over family. It's that simple.'

'There was nothing simple about it. Keep your voice down. People are looking at us, Marco.' She reached for her drink and her hair slid forward, framing her cheek. 'You chose to do this in a public place so can we at least try and keep this civilised?'

'Civilised?' Heat exploded inside him, the flame of his anger fuelled by her unreasonable calm. 'You ripped our marriage to shreds with your bare hands. Forgive me, *amore*, if I don't feel completely civilised. I feel—' He broke off, his fluency in English momentarily stunted by emotion, but before he could find the words to express his feelings she half rose to her feet.

'This conversation is pointless. I shouldn't have come.'

Grimly determined not to let her leave, Marco reached out a hand and caught her arm. 'Sit down. You're the one who wanted this conversation.'

'This isn't conversation, Marco, this is confrontation.' She was breathing quickly. 'You're losing your temper and I simply wanted us to discuss the facts.'

'I'm *not* losing my temper.' He drew in a breath, struggling to keep his tone level. 'I have a question.'

She sank back onto her chair, her beautiful eyes wary. 'What?'

'Do you think about us? About what we had? Have you forgotten what we shared?'

Her swift intake of breath and the brief flash of awareness in her eyes was sufficient answer. 'Marco—'

The phone in his pocket rang and he cursed fluently in Italian and slid it out of his pocket, wishing at that moment that he had chosen a different career path. One that would have permitted him five minutes' free time with the guarantee of no disturbance. He checked the number and sighed. 'That's Kate. She wouldn't ring unless it was important.'

'It's fine. Take the call.'

Frustrated that he'd been interrupted in what had to have been the most important part of the conversation, Marco hit the button and spoke to the practice manager, aware of Amy's eyes on his face.

Never before had he so badly wanted his work to go away.

And then Kate spoke and immediately she had his attention.

By the time he ended the call, Amy was no longer his priority.

She looked at him expectantly. 'Something bad?'

'The Knight boys have gone missing.' He rose to his feet. 'Eddie is only five years old.' He reached for his coat just as the door to the pub flew open and a little boy stood there, breathing hard.

'Dr Avanti! You have to come *now*! Alfie and I went to play on the rocks and Eddie followed because he always tags along and then he slipped and now we can't wake him up and he's bleeding everywhere and—' He broke off, his breath hitching as he spoke. 'We think he's dead, Dr Avanti. *He's dead!*'

CHAPTER FOUR

'*Calma*. Calm down, Sam.' Marco squeezed the boy's shoulder and squatted down so that he was level with him. 'Tell me where they are. Slowly.'

'We were playing pirates. Mum said we weren't to go near the rocks but we went anyway and Eddie followed and now...' Sam's face crumpled. 'He's dead. There's blood everywhere.'

Marco put an arm around the boy and spoke softly to him.

Amy couldn't hear what he said but it had a positive effect on Sam, who straightened his shoulders and stopped crying, his gaze trusting as he looked up at Marco. 'You mean that? Really?'

Marco nodded and let go of the boy. 'And now I want you to show me where they are.' He rose to his feet and noticed Amy. 'Stay here. Promise me you won't leave until we've finished this conversation.'

'I'm coming with you.'

Already on his way to the door with Sam, Marco frowned at her. 'I can't have a conversation while I'm administering first aid.'

'I'm coming to help you,' she said calmly. 'I'm a doctor, too, remember?'

Marco's jaw tensed. 'I thought you couldn't wait to leave

this place?' His tone was rough and his eyes scanned her briefly. 'You're not dressed to scramble down cliffs.'

'I'm fine. We're wasting time, Marco.'

'Hurry up or they'll have no blood left!' Sam was still in the doorway, his eyes huge and worried. 'I'll show you where they are.'

Marco glanced towards the bar. 'Tony—call the coast-guard and let them know what's happening. If it's serious we might need the helicopter to lift them off the rocks.'

Sam sprinted from the pub to the steep, narrow path that led down to the rocky cove below. 'Come on! Come on!' he urged them.

Amy didn't hear Marco's reply because she was too busy trying to keep her balance on the path. The wind had risen and now whipped her hair across her face, obscuring her vision. She knew just how steep the path was because it had been a favourite of hers as a child. The cove below was rocky and dangerous and held just the right amount of wicked appeal for an adventurous child.

Ahead of her, Marco covered the distance with sure, con-fident strides, drawing away from her, leaving her only the occasional reassuring glimpse of his broad shoulders.

She couldn't decide whether she was relieved or sorry that their conversation had been interrupted yet again.

It was obvious that Marco was equally frustrated by the interruptions. The question was whether he was frustrated enough to just agree to the divorce and let her walk out of Penhally before nightfall.

Did he believe her claim that she'd chosen a career over marriage and children?

Resisting the temptation to hurry because haste might result in her crashing onto the beach and becoming another casualty, Amy followed more slowly and finally clambered over the huge boulders that guarded the entrance to the cove. In the summer it was a favourite place for tourists who came with their nets and their buckets to explore the rock pools. In winter it was a wild and dangerous place and the sudden drop in the temperature had made the rocky beach particularly deadly.

Jagged rocks glistened black with sea spray and Amy glanced across and saw the boys. One lay still, the other sitting beside him, his face covered in blood.

Sam and Marco were already there and Amy picked her way across the rocks to join them.

'We didn't mean him to die. We didn't mean him to die. Do something, Dr Avanti,' Alfie whispered, his whole body shaking and juddering as he fixed his terrified stare on the inert form of his little brother. 'We didn't know he'd followed us and then I tried to take him back but he slipped and banged his head really hard. And when I tried to get to him, I slipped and hit my head, too. Then he stopped talking. I couldn't get him to answer me.' He started to sob pitifully and Sam started to cry, too. He caught Marco's eyes and took a shuddering breath.

'It will be all right, Alfie,' he said in a wobbly voice. 'We've got to be strong and try and help. What do you want us to do, Dr Avanti?'

Marco was on his knees beside the still body of the little boy. 'Just sit there for a moment, Sam. He isn't dead, Alfie. I can tell you for sure that he isn't dead.'

Amy knelt down beside Marco, wincing slightly as the sharp rocks took a bite out of her knees. 'Is he conscious?'

'No.' Marco was checking the child's scalp, nose and ears, searching for injury. And then the child gave a little moan and his eyes drifted open. 'All right. Well, that's good. He's drowsy. Obviously knocked out, from the boys' description.' His fingers probed gently. 'He's got a nasty haematoma on the back of his skull. I can't be sure that he doesn't have neck injuries.'

'Is he going to die?' Alfie's voice shook and Marco lifted his head and looked at him.

'No. He's not going to die.' His voice was firm and confident. 'You did the right thing to send Sam up to the pub. Good boy. Well done.'

Alfie looked at him, clearly doubtful that he'd done anything worthy of praise, and Amy noticed fresh blood oozing from the cut on his scalp.

'I'll ring the coastguard and then look at Alfie.' Amy started to dig for her phone but Marco shook his head.

'There's no signal on this beach. We can't carry him back up that path without possibly making things worse. Sam.' Marco's gaze slid to the other boy who was huddled next to Alfie, a look of terror in his eyes. 'I want you to go back up to the pub and tell Tony that we need a helicopter. Do you understand me?'

Sam shot to his feet and nodded, his face white and terrified. 'Helicopter. I can do that. I can do that, Dr Avanti.'

'Good boy. Go. And be careful on the rocks. We've had enough casualties here for one day.' Marco turned back to the child. 'Eddie? Can you hear me? He's cold, Amy. Wet from the sea and freezing in this weather. If we're not careful it's going to be hypothermia that is our biggest problem.' He cursed softly. 'I have no equipment. Nothing.'

Next to them, Alfie started to sob again, the tears mingling with the blood that already stained his cheeks. 'He's going to die. I know he's going to die. He chose me a really great Christmas present. I don't want him to die. This is all my fault. We're not supposed to be down on this beach anyway.'

Concerned about the amount of blood on Alfie's head, Amy made a soothing noise and examined his scalp. As she balanced on the slippery rocks, searching for the source of the bleeding, she suddenly developed a new admiration for para-medics. Then she saw blood blossom under her fingers and pulled off her gloves and took the scarf from her neck. 'I'm going to press on this for a minute, Alfie, and that should stop the bleeding. They can have a better look at it at the hospital.'

'I don't want to go to hospital. I want my mum—*Ow!*' Alfie winced. 'That really hurts.'

'You've cut yourself,' Amy murmured. 'I'm just going to put some pressure on it.'

'I don't care about me.' Alfie's eyes were fixed on his brother. 'If we'd stayed in the house it never would have happened. I wish we'd done that. I'm *never* playing on the beach again. I'm just going to stick to computers.' He sobbed and sobbed and Amy tightened the scarf and then slid her arms round him, cuddling him against her.

'It was just an accident, sweetheart,' she said softly. 'Accidents happen. Eddie's going to be all right, I know he is.'

Having examined Eddie as best he could, Marco removed his coat and pulled his jumper over his head. Then he wrapped the boy in the layers, giving him as much protection from the elements as possible. Then he glanced at Alfie and winked at him. 'Do you know how many accidents can happen sitting indoors, playing on the computer?'

Alfie sniffed, still clinging to Amy. 'Now you're kidding me.'

'You can have an accident without ever moving from your chair at home. The ceiling can drop onto your head. You can develop muscle strain and eye strain from too much gaming. Heart disease from lack of exercise. At least you were having fun outdoors.'

'But Eddie wouldn't have been here if it hadn't been for me. I chose the smugglers game. He loves dressing up as a pirate.'

'So—you're a fun brother to have and pirates sounds like a good game,' Marco said easily. 'You'll have to tell me more about it someday soon.' He glanced at Amy and gave a faint smile of approval as he saw her first-aid measures. 'Very inventive.'

'You learn to be inventive in Africa.' She pressed hard on the wound. 'They're not exactly flush with equipment over there.'

Something flickered in his eyes and then he turned his attention back to his little patient.

'Do we have to go to hospital?' Alfie's voice wobbled and he sounded very young. 'Our mum is going to go mad.'

'She'll just be relieved you're safe. Now, sit down here for a moment.' Amy helped him sit down on a flat piece of rock. 'Don't move. It's very slippery and I don't want you to fall again and I want to help Dr Avanti with your brother.'

Shivering without the protection of her scarf, she moved across to Marco and knelt down beside him. 'You must be frozen. You gave all your layers to Eddie.'

'I have more body fat than he does.'

Amy's eyes slid to his powerful, male frame. Not an inch of fat was visible. Just lean muscle under a thin T-shirt that clung to the impressive width of his shoulders. But she knew there was no point in pointing out that he was getting cold. Marco would do everything within his power to save a child. She'd always known that about him.

A hiss and a crash reminded her that the sea in winter was hungry and unforgiving and frighteningly close. 'That was a big wave, Marco.'

'Yes.' Marco's tone was matter-of-fact. 'If the helicopter doesn't arrive in the next few minutes, we might have to move him. I don't want to but it's the lesser of two evils.'

Amy glanced up at the sky, willing it to arrive.

Eddie gave a little whimper and Marco murmured something reassuring and tucked the layers more tightly around the child. 'He's in and out of consciousness. I should have asked Sam to bring blankets down from the pub.'

'The helicopter will be here before Sam gets back,' Amy said optimistically. 'I can give him one of my layers.' She started to take off her coat but he reached out and caught her arm.

'No.' This time his voice was harsh. 'Keep your coat on. You need it.'

'But—'

'Don't argue with me, Amy. You don't exactly have an excess of body fat to keep you warm. Didn't they feed you in Africa?'

She swallowed but was spared the trouble of thinking up an answer by the noise of the approaching helicopter.

'Good.' Marco watched with visible relief as the helicopter appeared in the sky like a giant insect. In a matter of minutes it was overhead and Amy could see the winchman in the doorway of the helicopter.

With precise, accurate flying and slick teamwork, the winchman was lowered onto the rocks next to them.

He unclipped the harness and moved across to them. 'How many casualties, Marco?'

Amy was wondering how they knew each other and then remembered that the RAF winchmen were trained paramedics who often practised their skills alongside local doctors.

'Two. One of them serious. According to his brother, he lost consciousness when he fell. GCS was 13 when we arrived on the scene...' Marco gave a swift, comprehensive summary of the situation and together they prepared Eddie for his transfer to hospital. Finally, strapped to a backboard, the child was winched into the helicopter.

Shivering like a wet puppy, Alfie watched. 'Wow!' His

voice was awed, concern for his little brother momentarily forgotten. 'That's so cool!'

Marco pulled on his jumper. 'It's definitely cool,' he murmured, helping the boy to his feet as the paramedic returned, ready to take his second patient.

'I'm going up there, too? Just wait until they hear about this at school.'

'Maybe he would have been safer on the computer,' Marco murmured, watching as the second child was safely winched into the helicopter. Then he lifted his hand in acknowledgement and the helicopter soared away on the short journey to hospital.

Around them the sea thrashed and boiled like a wild beast, angered that its prey had been snatched from its jaws.

Amy was shivering uncontrollably. 'Let's get moving,' she muttered, and was suddenly enveloped in warmth as Marco wrapped his coat around her.

'Wear this.'

'You can't give me your coat!' Protesting, she tried to shrug her way out of it but he was stronger than her and more determined.

'Put it on.' His voice rough, he fastened the coat as if she were a child and then gave a faint smile. 'It swamps you.'

'Well, you're bigger than me.'

His eyes darkened and she flushed and turned away, picking her way across the rocks back towards the path. She knew that he was bigger than her. She'd always been aware of his physical strength. It was one of the things that drew women to him.

At the top of the path a little crowd was waiting, including the boys' mother, Mary.

'I sent them to play in the garden because they've been on those wretched game machines all holiday and then when I went to call them for lunch, there was no sign of them.' She covered her mouth with her hand but the sobs still came. 'I guessed they'd gone to the beach and that Eddie had followed them. Everyone's saying that he's badly hurt—'

Without hesitation, Marco stepped forward and slid an arm around her shoulders. 'They are boys and they were playing,' he said, his accent thicker than usual. 'Alfie has a cut on his head, but nothing that a few stitches won't sort out. Eddie also banged his head…' He paused. 'From Alfie's description it sounds as though he might have been knocked out when he fell on the rocks. But he was starting to regain consciousness when we got to him and they've taken him to the hospital.'

'I need to get up there right away. I need to call my husband so that we can go to the hospital.' Trying to hold herself together, Mary fumbled in her bag for her phone, her hands shaking so much she dropped the bag twice. 'He's gone to help my brother take down a shed in his garden. It will take him ages to get back with the way the roads are.'

Marco stooped, picked up her bag and handed it to her. 'I'll take you in the Maserati.' He looked at his watch. 'I've got time to drive you and still be back in time for afternoon surgery. Tell your husband you'll meet him up there.'

Mary looked at him, her eyes swimming with tears. 'You'd do that for me?' She bit her lip. 'But there must be other more urgent things you should be doing.'

Marco looked directly at Amy and she knew what he was thinking. *That the thing he should be doing was giving her the conversation she'd demanded.*

So it was up to her, then, to decide. He was giving her the choice. She could insist that he stay and finish the conversation they'd started or she could let him take this frantic mother to her children.

'We can talk later,' she said quietly, slipping off his coat and handing it to him. 'My train doesn't leave until four.'

With only the briefest hesitation Marco reached into his pocket and gave his car keys to Mary. 'Go and sit in the car. I'll be with you in a minute.'

The woman walked across the car park and Amy gave a faint smile. 'Trusting someone else with your precious Maserati, Marco?'

'Only because I need to talk to you without an audience,' he growled, reaching out and removing a smudge of blood from her cheek. 'You're freezing and you need a shower. Go back to the surgery and ask Kate to sort you out with a change of clothes. Wait for me there. We'll talk later.'

'I think our conversation is doomed. We're running out of time.'

'Then stay overnight.'

She stared at him. 'That's out of the question.'

'I thought you wanted to talk? Stay the night, Amy, and then at least we're guaranteed peace and quiet. I'm not on call. You can come out to the house and we can eat, talk and then you can get the first train back tomorrow. I'll drop you at the station myself.'

'That's not—no.' She had to say no. 'I can't.'

'Amy.' His voice was impatient and he glanced towards his car where Mary was now waiting in a state of anxiety. 'We can't tie this up in a matter of minutes. We need time and we need privacy. You're the one who wants to do this. It makes sense. In fact, I can give you the house keys and you can go now and have a shower at home. That's a much better idea. Wait for me there. I'll be home by six and we can talk.'

She hadn't wanted to go to the house. It would just be too painful.

'I don't—'

'Stop arguing and looking for problems.' He dug in his pocket and pulled out his house keys. 'In that car is a woman worrying herself to death about her children and in the hospital are two young children who need their mother. They need my help and you're holding me up.'

Amy swallowed and took the keys from his hand. 'I'll see you later.'

Marco let himself into the house and walked through to the enormous sitting room that faced out to sea.

Amy was standing by the glass, staring out across the crashing waves. She was wearing the same soft wool trousers that she'd been wearing all day but she'd removed the rest of her soaked clothes and helped herself to one of his jumpers. The fact that it swamped her just increased the air of vulnerability that surrounded her.

She didn't turn when he entered the room but he could tell from the sudden increase in tension in her narrow shoulders that she was aware of his presence. 'The view is incredible.' Her voice was almost wistful. 'It was this room that sold me the house.'

Vulnerable, maybe, but still capable of wreaking havoc.

Engulfed by a fresh spurt of anger, Marco dropped his coat over the back of the sofa. 'It's a shame you didn't stay around long enough to live in it.'

She turned, pain in her eyes. 'Don't do this, Marco. This doesn't have to be an argument. Just let it go.'

'Like you did?' He watched her face, searching for some glimpse of the woman he'd married. 'You just let our relationship slip through your fingers. You never once tried to solve whatever problem it was that you suddenly found. You just walked away.'

Anguish flickered across her face and for a moment she looked as though she was going to defend herself. Then her shoulders sagged and she turned back to look out of the window as if she'd lost the will to fight. 'We wanted different things. You married me because you wanted to start a

family and at first I thought I wanted that, too.' She broke off
and sucked in a breath. 'But I discovered that I didn't. That
sort of difference is too big to bridge, Marco.'

He stared at her with mounting incredulity.

She made herself sound both flighty and indecisive and
neither adjective fitted what he knew about her. *Nothing she
said made sense.*

'So you had a sudden change of heart—why didn't you
discuss it with me?'

'There was nothing to discuss. You wanted one thing, I
wanted another.'

Marco tried to make sense of her words. She was saying
that she didn't want children and yet he'd seen her with
children and had been captivated by how gentle and kind she
was. Just now with Alfie, she'd been tactile and gentle. He'd
seen how much she cared. In fact, he would have said that she
was better with children than adults.

'You love children. You couldn't wait to be a mother,' he
said hoarsely. 'That's why I married you.'

'Yes.' This time when she turned to face him, her expression was blank. 'I know that's why you married me. And
that's why I knew that it would never work. I knew that there
was no point in "trying again" or working at our marriage.
There was no point in talking it through or having endless dis-
cussions that wouldn't have led anywhere. You married me
because you wanted to settle down and have a family. You
were perfectly clear about that. And I'm telling you right
now that that isn't what I want. So ending our marriage is the
fairest thing for both of us. You should be with a woman who
wants children. That's very important to you and you can't
ignore something like that.'

Marco inhaled sharply and laid himself bare. 'For me, you
were that woman, Amy. What was I to you?' *She wasn't good
at communicating but he'd thought he'd known what she'd*

*felt. He'd felt utterly secure in her love. Arrogance on his
part? Maybe.*

'You were—' She broke off and her eyes slid from his.
'You were a wonderful affair that never should have become
anything more.'

If he hadn't been so exasperated and confused he would
have laughed. 'You're trying to tell me you wanted the sex
and no commitment? Do you have any idea how ridiculous
that sounds, coming from you? You don't have affairs!' *It was
one of the reasons he'd wanted to marry her.*

'How would you know? We were only together for three
months before we married. That's not enough time to know
someone. You never really knew me, Marco.'

He'd *thought* he'd known her. 'I know you're not the sort
of woman to have a casual affair.'

'Maybe I *am* that sort of woman in some circumstances!
I'm not the first woman to find you irresistible, Marco. You're
an incredibly sexy guy. Intelligent, good company...' She
shrugged as if his attractions were so obvious it was pointless naming them. 'I don't suppose there's a woman in the
world who would reject you.'

He decided not to point out that *she* was rejecting him. 'So
now you're saying that I seduced you?'

'Of course not. I'm just saying that...the physical side
took over.'

'Physical? You married me because I'm good in bed? What
about the rest of our relationship?' Finding the entire conversation completely unfathomable and beginning to wonder
whether his English was less fluent than he'd previously
believed, Marco ran a hand over the back of his neck and held
on to his temper with difficulty. 'As I said before, we weren't
teenagers, Amy. Yes, there was strong chemistry but our minds
were working, too. We shared a great deal more than an incredible sex life.'

Colour bloomed in her cheeks and he remembered just how shy she'd been when they'd first met. 'We were friends, yes. But we never should have been more than that.'

'Was our relationship really that shallow? What about all those plans we made, or is my memory playing tricks? The way you're describing our life together…' he spread his hands in a gesture of raw frustration '…I'm beginning to think we're talking about a completely different relationship!'

'Perhaps we just saw it differently.'

'When we met you enjoyed your work, certainly, but your plans for the future were the same as mine. Family. We lay in bed and talked about having children. We agreed that I would work and you would stay at home with them. You thought it was important for a child to be with its mother, to know it was loved. These weren't *my* plans, *tesoro*, they were *our* plans.'

'To begin with, yes. But then I realised that it was never going to work.'

'Answer me one question, Amy. Did you love me?'

She froze and her eyes slid from his. 'No.' Her voice was so faint he could barely hear her. 'Not enough.'

Her answer shocked him so much that for a moment he didn't answer. *She'd loved him.* He *knew* that she'd loved him.

Or had he been deluding himself?

She'd left, hadn't she? She hadn't tried to mend their marriage. The only contact she'd had with him had been in relation to their separation. Were those the actions of a woman in love? No.

Which left him guilty of arrogance.

Just because attracting women had never been a problem in his life, he'd grown complacent.

He watched her for a moment, trying to make sense of it all—*searching again for the Amy he'd married.* 'So when did you first realise that you didn't love me enough?' The words almost stuck in his throat. 'Everything was fine until we moved back to Penhally. You seemed happy enough to begin with.' Scrolling through events in his mind, he watched her, still searching for clues. 'When did you suddenly decide that you wanted career, not family? And why didn't you share your thoughts with me?'

She turned back to the window. 'You were working, Marco—busy setting up the surgery with Nick. You were hardly ever home so it was hard to share anything with you. I was lonely. And I discovered that I missed working. I discovered that my own career was more important to me than I'd thought it was. Our relationship was so intense that for a short time I was totally infatuated with you. Babies—a family—that was all part of the same infatuation. But good, stable marriages aren't based on physical passion.'

Marco frowned. 'So when did you have this sudden change of heart? Not in the first few weeks, that's for sure. You spent your days going to estate agents because we both agreed we wanted a house out of town and preferably right on the cliffs. You dismissed three properties because they didn't have a garden. I still remember the day you rang me at work to tell me about this place. You were so excited! You'd even picked out the room that you thought should be the nursery. Where was the career woman then, Amy? *Where was she?*' He stared at her profile and saw the faint sheen of tears in her eyes.

The tears diluted his anger and he gave a soft curse and turned away from her, guilt tearing through him. '*Mi dispiace.* I'm sorry. Don't cry. Don't do that.' He hated it when women cried, although to be fair to her, she'd never done that to him before. He stared moodily down at the waves crashing onto the rocks, feeling as though his body and mind were under the same steady assault as the coastline. 'If you truly don't love me enough then there is nothing to be done.' This was entirely new territory for him. In the past he'd been the one to tell a woman that a relationship was over—*that he didn't love her enough.*

Only now was he discovering that it wasn't an easy thing to hear.

He glanced towards her and wondered why, if she didn't love him, she looked so utterly, utterly lost and miserable. 'You've changed so much.'

'Perhaps I have. Didn't you always say that women are sometimes difficult to understand? That we think in different ways?'

Marco gave a twisted smile, bitterly amused at his own arrogance. To think that he'd once thought that he understood women. Amy had long since proved that not to be the case. 'So, after two years of thinking in your very different way, you decided to turn up and ask for a divorce.'

'We've been apart for two years.'

'And that's some sort of magic figure? If you were expecting me to smile and sign, you picked the wrong man to marry and divorce.' His mouth tightened. 'Perhaps I should have mentioned this before, but I don't believe in divorce.'

'Surely that depends on the marriage. You don't want to be married to someone who doesn't love you. It's time to get on with our lives, Marco. I can pursue my career. You can find someone else. You can marry someone else who will give you a whole houseful of children.'

Was that what he wanted?

He'd only ever imagined this house full of his and Amy's children. *Did he want children with another woman?*

CHAPTER FIVE

THE phone rang and Marco let out a stream of Italian, clearly incensed at being interrupted yet again. His eyes glittered dangerously and he glared at the phone as if his anger alone should be enough to silence it.

'Answer it, Marco,' Amy said wearily. 'It's probably someone else whose life needs saving.'

He was angry with her. *So angry with her.*

And intellectually he was outmanoeuvring her at every step, pouncing on holes in her argument like the most ruthless trial lawyer. And there were plenty of holes. Her defence was thin and full of inconsistencies, she knew that, but she hadn't expected to be on trial long enough for it to matter. She'd expected a quick conversation and a rapid exit. She hadn't expected him to argue with her.

She hadn't expected him to *care* enough to argue and she certainly hadn't expected him to ask if she'd loved him.

That had been the most difficult lie of all.

And what now? Was he going to let her go?

Was he going to find another woman to share his heart and have his children?

The thought of another woman living in this house, living with Marco, brought a lump to her throat.

She wasn't going to think about that right now.

Grateful for the brief respite offered by the phone, she watched as he strode across the room and lifted the handset, his movements purposeful. He was a man who was focused and didn't waste time, hence the reason he was able to cope with such a punishing workload without crumbling under the pressure.

'Nick? Problems?' He didn't even bother to disguise his impatience at the interruption and Amy winced slightly, wondering what the senior partner in the practice was thinking about her sudden unexpected return. Was he cursing her for distracting his partner when they were so busy?

It was obvious from the conversation that Nick was asking Marco about a patient and Marco sprawled into the nearest chair and gave the information that was needed.

He was never given any peace, Amy thought to herself, listening as he and Nick debated different courses of action. But he never tried to hide from his responsibilities. From the moment he'd decided to set up the surgery in Penhally with Nick, he'd been dedicated to delivering the very best health care to the local population. He was that sort of man.

The sort of man who would be an amazing father.

Feeling slightly sick, Amy tried to subdue the misery that bubbled up inside her. *Not now.* She wasn't going to think about that now. She dare not. Marco was far too astute. She had to make it look as though this was what she wanted.

'Amy?' The conversation concluded, he replaced the phone and looked at her. 'Sorry for the interruption. Since Lucy left it's been crazy. The snow hasn't helped. No one is used to having snow in the village and everyone is slipping on pavements and injuring themselves.' He ran a hand over his face. 'And it's New Year's Eve in a few days' time.'

Amy knew from experience that New Year's Eve was always busy for the local health team and being one doctor down would be a problem. 'You haven't managed to find anyone to cover Lucy?'

'We weren't exactly expecting her to deliver so early. We didn't have time to arrange locum cover. Kate is still working on it.' He leaned his head back against the sofa and closed his eyes. His dark lashes brushed the hard, strong lines of his cheekbones and Amy stared hungrily.

The early morning had always been her favourite time of day, when he had still been asleep and she'd been able to just study his face without having to worry about what she was revealing.

'She told me this afternoon that she may have found someone, but he can't start for another month. Until then it's all hands on deck, except that the ship is sinking. I haven't even asked—how was surgery this morning?' He opened his eyes suddenly and she coloured, embarrassed that he'd caught her looking at him.

'Surgery was interesting.' *Talking about work was good.* 'Along with the usual coughs, colds and sore throats, I saw my first ever case of erysipelas and a case of ophthalmic shingles.'

'I suppose the erysipelas was one of the trawlermen; it usually is. Ophthalmic shingles?' He raised an eyebrow. 'Who was that?'

'A Mrs Duncan?'

'Paula? She's a writer. Detective novels, I think. Lives in that white house on the cliffs. You're sure it was shingles?'

Astonished that he knew so much about his patients, Amy nodded. 'Yes, she had all the symptoms and skin lesions on the side of her nose.'

'Did you refer her to the hospital?'

'Yes.'

'Poor Paula. That's the last thing she needs over the Christmas holidays. Did you give her oral aciclovir? Eight hundred milligrams?'

Amy sighed. 'Marco, if you're so worried about my skills, don't ask me to take your surgery.'

'Sorry.' He gave a faint smile, the first smile that had touched his mouth since she'd walked back into his life that morning. 'I'm not used to delegating. And especially not to my wife.' He studied her for a moment, his dark eyes narrowed and his long legs stretched out in front of him. He looked impossibly sexy and Amy's mouth dried and she turned away from him, her heart thudding hard against her chest.

'Well—it was just the one surgery,' she muttered, feeling his gaze burning a hole between her shoulder blades.

'So what are your plans once you finally catch that train? Are you returning to Africa or are they sending you somewhere else?'

'I don't know. They've asked me to go to Pakistan.'

'But you haven't accepted?'

'Not yet.' She turned, wondering where the conversation was going. 'I wanted to get things sorted out here first.'

Marco held her gaze. 'So you're out of a job. You, who love work above everything else.' It was impossible to miss the sarcasm in his voice and Amy's tongue tied itself in a knot.

'I'm not exactly out of work.' She tried to retrace her steps. 'I'll go where I'm needed.'

'Is that right? In that case I have a proposition for you. You stay in Penhally for a month. Work in the practice. You've probably noticed that we're struggling. Nick, Dragan and I can't keep it going on our own.'

Amy stared at him for a moment, wondering if she'd misheard. 'That's out of the question.'

'Why? You've just said that you'll go where you're needed. You're needed here, Amy.'

'No.'

'You keep telling me how important it is for you to work. We need another doctor in Penhally. Urgently. You're good at what you do and you're capable of just stepping in and getting on with things. You proved that this morning. If you hadn't been here, surgery would have ground to a halt.'

'You don't want your ex-wife working in your practice.'

'My *wife*.' He emphasised the word gently. 'Actually, you're my *wife*, Amy, not my ex-wife. And why is that a problem? If you don't love me then there are no emotions involved, so working together should be easy. It's a good solution.'

Not for her.

Amy stood there in a blind panic, once again trapped by her own words. 'That's a ridiculous suggestion. We can't work together.'

'Why not?'

Because it would be too painful. *Because she wouldn't be able to hide her true feelings.* 'Marco, don't do this.'

'Don't do what? Don't talk sense? We need a doctor, you need a job. You don't love me—fine, we work together as friends and colleagues and at the end of a month I give you that divorce you want. One month, working side by side as we've done today.'

So basically she had to allow herself to be tortured for a month in order to achieve something that she didn't really want anyway.

She almost laughed.

'It would be too…awkward. Marco, how can you even suggest it?'

'We are both mature, professional people. Why would it be awkward? The only possible reason for it to be awkward would be if you still felt something for me. Is that the case, Amy? Do you feel something?'

It was like being in court in front of a deceptively gentle prosecutor determined to dig up the truth. 'I don't— That isn't what I mean.' She stumbled over the words. 'I don't feel anything for you, Marco. I'm sorry if that's hurtful but it's better that I tell the truth.'

'*Are* you telling the truth?' He was watching her closely, his gaze disturbingly intense. 'There's something going on here, Amy. Something that isn't right.'

'You're putting me in an impossible position, that's what isn't right! I can't stay, Marco.'

'Why not?' There was a hard edge to his tone. 'You've said that you never loved me and that our relationship was just a fling. Since when did a bit of hot sex need to get in the way of a sensible business arrangement? Work is all-important to you and I'm offering you work. If emotions aren't involved, there can't be a problem, can there?'

Her emotions *were* involved. But to admit that would be to admit that she was still in love with him and that would lead to complications that she couldn't handle.

Amy waded through her options and found them depressingly limited. It was obvious that if she refused he would take her refusal as an indication that she was in love with him and she just didn't want him knowing that.

Desperate now, she searched for another excuse—*anything*—that might help her extricate herself from the situation. 'I only planned to come for the day. I don't have clothes or anything.'

'All your clothes are still here. Upstairs in the wardrobe where you left them.' His tone was even. 'In case you've forgotten, you didn't take much with you.'

She'd been too upset to even bother with packing.

Amy turned away and walked over the window, her mind racing. Unlike him, she wasn't thinking clearly.

She could walk away, but then she'd just have to come back and go through all this again another time. Or she could stay and work in Penhally and prove that their relationship was truly over.

All she had to do was keep up the act for a month and then he'd give her a divorce.

She stared out to sea, watching the waves rise and fall. It wasn't as if they'd see that much of each other, she reasoned. She'd already seen how much of his life was tied up with the practice. They'd both be working. She wouldn't be spending a lot of time in his company.

How hard would it be?

'You're joining us?' Nick Tremayne stared at Amy across the desk, a serious expression on his face. 'You're going to work as a locum?'

'Just until Dr Donnelly arrives. Kate has confirmed that he can start in a month.' Exhausted after a sleepless night in Marco's spare room, Amy summoned up a smile that she hoped reflected the correct amount of enthusiasm for the situation. 'I took Marco's surgery for a while yesterday morning and I enjoyed it. I'm between jobs at the moment and you're stuck so it seemed a sensible solution.' *Did she sound convincing?*

Probably not, given that she wasn't entirely convinced herself.

But Marco had pushed so relentlessly that she'd found herself trapped between all the lies she'd told.

Nick looked at her, his gaze just a little too probing for her liking. 'I hate to point out the obvious…' he glanced towards Marco '…but you guys haven't seen each other for two years. Much as we need the help professionally, I can't risk the problems of your personal life invading practice business.'

'We're very civilised,' Marco said easily. 'Working together won't be a problem.'

Wouldn't it? Unconvinced, Amy glanced at him, trying to read his mind, but his face gave nothing away. *Was he really as relaxed about the whole thing as he seemed?*

Perhaps Nick was asking himself the same question because he studied his friend and colleague for a moment before turning back to Amy. 'Where are you going to live?'

Amy opened her mouth to reply but Marco was there first. 'In the house, with me. Where else? I'm rattling around with five bedrooms.' His emphasis on the word 'five' could have been a linguistic slip or else a gentle reminder that they'd chosen the house with the intention of filling it with their children. 'Amy missed her train so she stayed last night. We managed to get through the night without killing each other so I don't anticipate a problem.'

He was expecting her to live in the same house as him? No! That hadn't been part of the original plan. She'd been banking on the fact that, apart from the odd bit of professional communication at work, she'd be able to avoid him. Yes, she'd stayed the previous night—shivering in the spare room like an interloper—but she'd assumed that she'd be finding herself alternative accommodation at some point. Already her eyes were gritty and her head ached as a result of a night in his spare bedroom. She'd spent the entire night awake, imagining Marco just next door, probably sprawled naked in the enormous bed that they'd chosen for the main bedroom, and now she discovered that she was going to be staying there every night.

Amy opened her mouth to argue and then caught Nick's searching look and instead smiled weakly. Thanks to Marco's confident announcement she now had no choice but to stay with him. 'That's right,' she said hoarsely. 'I'm staying with him. No problem.'

Nick shrugged. 'Well, if you both think you can handle it. God knows, we need another doctor badly so I'm not likely to put up much of an argument. Welcome back, Amy, and welcome on board.' His tone was brisk. 'Well, this is a good start to the New Year. I was starting to think we might have a nervous breakdown before we found anyone to cover Lucy's maternity leave.'

'How is Lucy?' Amy tried to ignore the heavy feeling of dread that sat in her stomach. 'Is she doing all right?'

'Very well, considering the baby was premature. Annabel is still in Special Care but they're hoping to be back home for New Year.' Nick tapped his fingers on the desk, his expression thoughtful. It was clear that he was already planning, his mind on the practice and the needs of the local population. 'So, Amy, it's pretty obvious that you should just take on Lucy's patients and the antenatal clinic. I seem to remember that obstetrics was always your big love so it makes sense.'

Amy's mouth dried. 'No!' Forgetting all about the sleeping arrangements, she shook her head. 'No. I mean…could I do one of the other clinics?' *Not antenatal. Please, God, not that. Not now.* 'It would be great to do something different. Don't you do the antenatal clinic? I'd hate to take it away from you.' Aware that Marco was looking at her in astonishment, she tried to recover herself but Nick was frowning, too.

'Since Lucy left I've had to cover the minor surgery and I can't do it all. Marco does child health, of course, and Alison Myers, our practice nurse, does a fair few clinics on her own with no help. Dragan has other responsibilities that take him further afield, so he can't take on obstetrics.' Nick narrowed his eyes, studying her face carefully. 'You love obstetrics. Pregnant women were always your special interest. What's the problem? Is it something to do with your stint in Africa? I mean, it's not as if you're going to be expected to deliver the babies or anything. Just deliver the antenatal care. Have you had a drama that we ought to know about?'

'No. Nothing like that.' Her heart was galloping and her palms were damp. 'There's no problem, really,' she lied, her voice barely working. 'I just thought maybe it would be better to have a more permanent doctor doing that particular clinic. For continuity. Women like continuity, don't they?'

She wished Marco would stop looking at her. And now Nick was looking at her, too. And she had a feeling that the older doctor would be asking her questions sooner rather than later.

'Ideally, yes,' Nick said slowly, his gaze intent on her face. 'But in this case I think they'll just be delighted to have a female doctor with expertise in obstetrics. I can't imagine that anyone is going to protest.'

She was protesting. But now they were both staring at her and she knew that she'd already betrayed far too much.

'Well, if you're sure they won't mind—I'll do the clinic, of course.' She gave what she hoped was a casual smile. 'It will be fine.' Fine. Fine. Fine. She was a trained professional. She could deliver whatever medical care was required of her.

She could do antenatal.

She could switch off. Shut down her feelings. Wasn't that what she'd done for the past two years?

'Good.' Nick's eyes lingered on her face for a moment longer and then he turned back to Marco. 'So that's decided, then. I'll tell Kate and she can inform the patients. Good news. Thanks, Amy. A timely arrival on your part if ever there was one. Lucky for us.'

Not lucky, Amy thought miserably, biting her lip so hard that she tasted blood. *Not lucky at all.*

'All right, so what the hell is happening between you and Amy? Is this happy ever after?' Nick hooked his hands behind his head and rocked back on his chair. 'Are the two of you back together?'

Marco lounged in the chair opposite, his expression guarded. 'Are you asking as my friend or my colleague?'

'What difference does it make? It's a simple yes or no answer.'

'We're not back together again...' Marco paused. 'Yet.'

'But you're working on it. It's what you want, obviously.' Nick made an impatient sound. 'What about Amy? The two of you were good together. What the hell is going on? I never really understood why she left in the first place.'

Marco kept his response factual. 'Apparently she wanted a career instead of children.'

'*Amy?*' Nick looked at him in disbelief. 'That doesn't sound right. She was very excited about starting a family. I remember catching her staring at a baby outfit in a shop window one day. She went a deep shade of scarlet but she had that look in her eyes. That look that warns you to go out and buy a people carrier.'

Marco didn't laugh. 'Well, the look has disappeared. It isn't what she wants any more. She doesn't want babies and she doesn't want me.'

'I wonder why not.'

'She doesn't love me enough.' Marco gave what he hoped passed as a casual shrug. 'It happens.'

Nick laughed with genuine amusement. 'But not to you. Women always love you. It's the accent and the dark, brooding eyes. Come on, Marco! What's the matter with you? Amy loves you! Anyone can see that. She isn't a woman who is fickle in her affections! She's a one-man woman and you're that man. You always have been.'

'Apparently not.' Feeling suddenly irritable, Marco rose to his feet. 'Was there anything else we needed to talk about? Because my love life has run its course as a topic of conversation.'

'How's the car? Did you get the Maserati fixed?'

'Yesterday. Kate arranged it.'

The change in Nick's expression was barely perceptible. 'She's a wonderfully efficient practice manager.'

And she was willing to be a great deal more if Nick would only give her some encouragement, Marco thought, wondering if his colleague was truly as obtuse about Kate's feelings as he pretended to be. Or was it much more complicated than that? Was he still churned up and guilty about the death of his wife? Unable to commit to anyone else?

Marco gave a mental shrug and decided not to pursue the subject. He had enough problems of his own in that department and he certainly wasn't in a position to lecture other people on how to run their love lives. 'I've put Amy in Lucy's consulting room. I assume that's all right with you.'

'As long as she's seeing patients I don't care if she's doing it from the toilet,' Nick drawled. Then he leaned forward. 'Any idea why she was so reluctant to run the antenatal clinic?'

'She doesn't really want to be here at all.' Marco gave a grim smile. 'I used some psychological leverage to get us a doctor for a few weeks. She's here under duress, I'm afraid.'

'Well, I guessed that.' Nick frowned and tapped his pen on the desk. 'But I had a feeling that there might be something more going on. She looked...distraught at the thought of doing that clinic. Pale. Ill. Maybe she's just tired.'

Marco felt a flicker of unease. 'Yes, I think something is wrong, too. That's why I want her to stay. Once I find out what it is and help her solve it, I'll let her go. Perhaps the problem is just that she wants to be as far away from me as is humanly possible.'

'It could be that. But she's a woman...' Nick flicked the switch on his computer '...which also means that it's likely to be something a million times more complicated than that. Watch her, Marco. There's something going on. Just don't let your personal life affect the practice.'

Marco tensed and his voice was a low growl. 'I don't need that lecture from you.'

'Good.' Nick gave a cool smile. 'Then I won't give it.'

'He's getting these headaches,' the woman said, pulling the little boy onto her lap. 'Always behind the left eye and he says it's like a drilling pain.'

Amy glanced at the child's notes, checking that there was nothing in his history that she should know about. 'And what's he like when he gets the headache, Sue? Can he still play or does he have to go and lie down?'

'I give him paracetamol syrup and he lies down. Then he's generally up and playing within about an hour and a half. The syrup works really well.'

Amy turned to the child. 'And when you have your bad headache, Harry, do you feel sick?'

'Sometimes I feel a bit churny in my stomach.'

'A bit churny.' Smiling at the description, Amy gave a sympathetic nod. 'Are you actually sick?'

'No, but when it happens at school they give me a bowl, just in case.'

Amy looked at Sue. 'And how long has he been getting headaches?'

'It's hard to say.' Sue bit her lip. 'I mean, children get headaches, don't they, so I didn't really think about it at first. Then it became more frequent and when he gets them he's sobbing and crying and it's quite scary. And I started to think—I mean—you're going to think I'm completely paranoid. A headache is just a headache isn't it? It's just that—' She broke off and glanced at the boy, clearly concerned about saying too much in front of him.

Amy leaned forward and wrote on a piece of paper. Then she leaned forward and gave it to the child. 'Harry, would you be kind enough to take this to the lady behind Reception for me? And then come back here. Thank you, sweetheart. That's really helpful.'

Eager to please, Harry left the room and Amy turned to the mother. 'I sense that there are things that you don't want to say in front of him.'

'Well, I don't want to worry him. And I'm probably just being paranoid but it's hard not to be with my history. I was diagnosed with bowel cancer two years ago and everyone told me that it couldn't possibly be anything serious. And then it was. I've had chemo and operations and—well, it's been really, really hard. And it makes you realise that things go wrong. People say, "Oh, it won't be anything," but that's what they said about me and they were wrong. It *was* something. And when that happens you can't just look at a headache and think headache, can you? I try and do that and all the time I'm thinking brain tumour.'

'You're not alone in that and you have more reason than most to worry, given everything that has happened,' Amy said softly, feeling her heart twist with sympathy. 'You've obviously had a terrible time. I'm so sorry.'

'It's not too bad now, things have gone quiet. But now this.' Sue looked at Amy and her eyes filled. 'I can cope with anything that happens to me but if anything happens to my child—to Harry—that's it, I'm telling you that now. That's it for me. No more. If my baby is ill, then I'll…' Tears poured down her cheeks and Amy reached out and gave her hand a squeeze.

'It is very unlikely that this is anything serious, but I can understand why you're worried, so this is what we're going to do. We're going to take a very, very good look at him and if necessary we'll refer him to the paediatrician for a specialist opinion. Anything we need to do to reassure you.'

'And how long will that take?' Sue reached into her bag for a tissue and blew her nose hard. 'I'm not sleeping at night because I'm so worried.'

The door opened and Harry bounced back into the room. 'She said, "thank you."'

Sue immediately pulled herself together, her smile just a little too bright as she scrunched up the tissue and pushed it up her sleeve. 'Good boy.'

'Yes, thank you, Harry.' Amy smiled and then turned back to Sue. 'Let's start by taking some history. Does anyone in the family suffer from migraines?'

'My mother and my sister. But not for years. I did take Harry to have his eyes tested because I thought it might be that, but the optician said that his eyes are fine. I brought you the report, just in case you wanted to see it.' She rummaged in her bag and pulled out a piece of paper.

Amy glanced at the results and nodded. 'Yes, they're fine. Nothing there that should cause a headache.' She asked a few more questions, recorded the answers carefully and then smiled at the boy. 'Hop on my couch, Harry, and I'll take a look at you.'

She examined the child thoroughly, found nothing that alarmed her but saw the desperate worry in Sue's eyes.

Amy thought for a moment. 'Sue, I can't find anything that would lead me to believe this is anything other than a straight-forward headache, but given your history I think it would be reassuring for you to have a second opinion. Dr Avanti is a qualified paediatrician, as you know. I think what we might do, given how worried you are, is to ask him to take a look at Harry.'

'Would he have time?'

Amy looked at the clock. 'Well, it's the end of surgery so let me just pop in and ask him and see how he's fixed.'

She left the room and found Marco in his consulting room, talking on the phone. He waved a hand towards a chair, finished the conversation and then looked at her expectantly. 'Problems?'

'I have Sue Miller in my room.'

'Sue?' His gaze sharpened. 'What's the matter with her? She was diagnosed with colorectal cancer a couple of years ago. I know Lucy did some follow-up with her.'

Amy looked at him curiously. 'Do you know everyone's patients?'

'*Sì*, if they have a history of serious illness, it's my business to know. It's important that all the partners are aware of what

is going on.' He shrugged. 'She was discussed in a practice
meeting a while ago. She's always a priority patient for us.
So, why is she seeing you today?'

'It isn't about her. It's about Harry. He's seven and he's
been having headaches.'

Marco gave a slow nod. 'And she thinks this is symptom-
atic of a brain tumour, no? I'm sure she is very anxious.'

'Exactly. Understandable in the circumstances.'

'Of course. And you've examined him?'

'Yes. I can't find anything, but I can see that she's very
worried. I could always refer her to a paediatrician, but that
would take time and given that you are a paediatrician, I
thought you might look at him for me. Provide instant reassurance.' She frowned. 'Always assuming that there *isn't*
anything to worry about.'

'Now who is being paranoid?' Marco said softly, a faint
flicker of humour in his eyes. 'Less than one per cent of headaches are caused by a brain tumour. I think you know that
statistic.'

'Yes.' Amy gave herself a little shake. 'But try telling that
to a thirty-five-year-old woman who developed cancer when
she shouldn't have done. I don't think she's a big believer in
the relevance of statistics.'

'Point taken. Of course I will see him. Your room or mine?'

His voice was silky smooth and Amy felt the colour flood
into her cheeks and cursed herself for reacting so strongly.
Why couldn't she be indifferent? Why?

'You may as well come to my room. Harry is playing
happily and it might be less unsettling for him.'

Marco picked up his stethoscope and auriscope and
followed her out of the room.

'By the way…' He paused outside the door. 'They're
having a New Year's Eve party at the Penhally Arms. We're
both invited.'

'Thanks, but no.' Amy shook her head. 'I'm here to work, not to party. You go. I'll stay at home and catch up on some paperwork.'

'You need to be there. You're a member of the community now. You need to make a showing.'

'I'm only here for a short time.'

'If you don't go, people will say that we're afraid to be seen together. We need to present a united front. They don't want to think that there's dissent at the surgery.'

Feeling trapped once again, Amy paused with her hand on the door. 'I can't go to a party with you, Marco.'

'Why not?' He looked genuinely puzzled. 'We're friends and colleagues. Why wouldn't you? We can spend a pleasant evening together. What's the problem? Let's go and take a look at Harry.' And he pushed open the door of her consulting room and walked inside, leaving her staring after him with frustration.

CHAPTER SIX

HE ALWAYS seemed to get his own way.

She'd come to Penhally planning to stay for an hour and here she was, working in the surgery, living with him in their old house and now contemplating going to a party with him. It was ridiculous!

Amy watched as he spoke quietly to Sue and then dropped into a crouch next to Harry.

'Hi, there, Harry.' His voice was good-humoured. 'Good Christmas? What did Father Christmas bring?'

'The most *amazing* remote-control car. You should see it, Dr Avanti, it's so cool.'

'You didn't bring it with you?' When Harry shook his head, Marco looked disappointed. 'Shame. Never mind. Next time I see you perhaps you'll have it with you.' He asked Harry a few questions and then did the same of Sue. 'I'm going to take a look at you, Harry. Can you take off your jumper and shirt and sit on that couch, please?'

Marco listened to the child's heart and lungs and then laid him down and examined his abdomen. 'How long have you been at your school, Harry?'

'Oh…' The boy thought for a moment. 'Pretty much my whole life.'

'Since nursery,' Sue muttered, a soft smile on her face as she looked at her child. 'Age four.'

Marco felt the femoral pulse. 'And who lives at home with you?'

'Well, my mum mostly.' Harry wrinkled his nose thoughtfully. 'And my dad comes home in the evenings.'

'Because he's at work all day,' Sue interjected hastily, and Marco smiled.

'Children are very literal. Any brothers or sisters, Harry?'

'Just Beth. She's two. She doesn't say much but she bites a lot. I suppose she's all right.' Harry looked a bit unsure on that point and Sue gave him a quick hug.

'She doesn't mean to bite, sweetheart. She's very little and her teeth are hurting.' She gave Marco an apologetic look. 'Beth is going through a biting phase at the moment. I'm talking to the health visitor about her in clinic next week.'

'Good idea.' Marco picked up the patella hammer and gently rolled up Harry's trouser leg. 'And what's your favourite subject at school?'

'Science.' Harry giggled as his leg jumped. 'Are you going to break my leg?'

'Definitely not.' Marco smiled and tested the reflexes in the child's feet. 'Doctors don't break legs, they fix them. Do you like your school, Harry? Are you happy?'

'Yes. Except for the lunches. The lunches are gross.'

'What do they give you for lunch?'

'Slugs and snails.'

Marco looked interested. 'Cooked or raw?'

Amy smiled. He was so good with children and they just adored him.

Harry was giggling. 'And worms. They call it spaghetti but it's *definitely* worms.'

'In Italy, where I come from...' Marco picked up the

child's T-shirt and handed it to him '…we eat a lot of worms. You can get dressed now.'

'You eat worms?' Harry shuddered and pulled on his clothes. 'Weird.'

'Very weird,' Marco agreed. 'Now, I want you to sit up and play a few games with me.'

'Games? Cool.' Harry sat up cheerfully, his legs dangling over the edge of the trolley, his expression enthusiastic. 'Now what?'

Marco stood in front of him, legs planted firmly apart, supremely confident. 'I want you to touch my finger and then touch your nose—that's good. And now with the other hand. Faster. Oh, you're good at that.'

'It's easy.'

'Now look at me.' Marco held his hand to the right of the boy's head and wiggled his finger. 'Tell me if my finger is moving or still.'

'Moving.'

'And now?'

'Still.'

Marco switched sides, performed a few more tests and then reached for the ophthalmoscope. 'And now I want to look in the back of your eyes. Amy, can you close the curtains for me, please? Look straight ahead at the picture on the wall, Harry. Keep looking at it even if I get in the way.' He examined the back of both eyes and then put the ophthalmoscope down and drew the curtains.

'Can you see my brain with that light?'

Marco smiled. 'Not your brain exactly but the back of your eye tells me things about your brain. Now put your arms up.' He carried on with the examination while Sue watched anxiously and Amy watched with interest. 'Sit on the floor for me, Harry.'

Eager to please, the little boy slid off the couch and sat on the floor. 'This is fun. Now what?'

'Now stand up as fast as you can.'

The boy leapt to his feet. 'I'm the quickest at gym.'

'I can see that.' Marco walked across to him, putting his heel directly in front of his other foot. 'Can you do this? It's like walking on a tightrope.'

'You mean like in the circus?' Harry chuckled and walked, arms outstretched like an acrobat. 'Like this?'

'Perfect. You're good at that. Better than me. So—we're finished. Good boy.' Marco sat down in the chair opposite Sue. 'All right. I don't see anything that worries me. I don't think this is what you're afraid it is, but if you want more definite reassurance I can refer him for an MRI scan.'

Sue pulled a face. 'I was scanned so many times. I wouldn't want him to have that. It's radiation, isn't it?'

'You're talking about CT scans. An MRI scan is different.' Marco's voice was calm and patient. 'There is no radioactivity, no risk to the patient and Harry is old enough to tolerate it with no problem.'

Sue looked at him and her eyes filled. 'You don't think it's…anything? Truly?'

Amy knew she was avoiding saying the word 'cancer' because the little boy was still in the room.

'I don't think so, although medicine is never an exact science, as you are well aware.' Marco's sympathetic smile indicated that he was referring to her own medical history. 'I think Harry might be suffering from migraines. Not an easy diagnosis to make in a child because the pattern of headaches is not always predictable, but what you describe—the drilling pain, the very definite episode, which is relieved by paracetamol, the fact he needs to lie down…' Marco shrugged his shoulders. 'This sounds to me like migraine and there is some family history to support the theory.'

Sue looked at him. 'If he were your child, what would you do?'

Amy felt her stomach flip. *Marco's child.*

His mind clearly in tune with hers, Marco's gaze flickered to hers momentarily and something burned, slow and hot, in the depths of his eyes. Amy swallowed, knowing that he was thinking of the plans they'd made to have a family.

'If he were mine...' Marco dragged his gaze from Amy's and glanced across at the little boy, who was playing happily on the carpet. 'If he were mine, I would watch him for a while, see how he goes. I think you should keep a diary of the headaches so that we can assess exactly how many he is getting, how long they last and whether there are any obvious triggers. Do that for six weeks and then make an appointment with one of us to go through the diary. We can look at the frequency and decide whether to refer him to the paediatricians at the hospital for them to take a closer look.'

'But you don't think—'

'No.' Marco's voice was firm. 'I don't. But we will watch him. And if you decide that you would be happier if he had an MRI scan, you have only to let me know and I will arrange it.'

Sue closed her eyes for a moment and let out a long breath. 'Thank you for that. I'll pass on the scan for the time being. But what could be causing the migraines, do you think?'

'It's hard to say.' Marco watched the child play. 'Often we underestimate children, especially very young children. We imagine that because they are young, they are somehow not aware of what is going on around them, but that is rarely the case. Most children are extremely intuitive and even if they don't pick up on conversations they pick up on atmosphere. Is he a sensitive child, would you say?'

'Very.' Sue looked at her son. 'He's a worrier. And very caring. Even in the playground at school, he's always watching out for other children.'

Marco nodded slowly. 'So—we know that the past two years have been very hard for you personally and also for your family. It would be almost impossible for that not to have had an impact.'

'I suppose so. We've done our best to protect the children, but inevitably some of it filters through.' Sue rose to her feet and managed a smile. 'But things are going better now. I'm hoping this is going to be our lucky year. Will you be in the Penhally Arms on New Year's Eve, Dr Avanti? I hear they're planning quite an evening.'

'*Sì*. Where else would I be on New Year's Eve when the drink is free?' Marco winked at her. 'I'll be there.'

'Then we might see you. Thank you, both of you. Harry…' Sue held out a hand to her son. 'Let's go and write a few more thank-you letters for all those Christmas presents.'

Harry gave an exaggerated shudder but followed his mother out of the room with a wave at Marco.

'Sweet boy,' Amy said quietly, and then realised that Marco was watching her.

'I thought you didn't like children?'

She stiffened. 'I never said I didn't like children. I just said I didn't want any of my own. That's completely different.' Uncomfortable under his scrutiny, she turned away. *She couldn't live like this.* Couldn't be on her guard the whole time. It was exhausting and she was a useless, terrible liar. 'So we'll keep an eye on him, then. Thanks for looking at him. You really think he's all right?'

'Who?' It was as if his mind was somewhere else entirely. Then he sighed. 'Oh, Harry—yes. Amy, his neurological examination was normal, there was no evidence of poor co-ordination, ataxia or nystagmus. His peripheral nervous system was normal. His cardiovascular system was normal. Personally, I wouldn't even scan him, but if Sue carries on worrying, it's worth arranging it.'

'I'll do that. Or I suppose the locum can do it if I've gone. I'll make sure the notes are detailed. Thank you, Marco.'

He studied her in brooding silence. 'My pleasure.'

The antenatal clinic was held that afternoon and Amy spent her entire lunch hour wondering whether there was any way she could get out of it without drawing attention to herself.

Five minutes before it was due to start she was still sitting in the staffroom when Kate hurried in. 'You haven't forgotten your clinic, Amy?'

If only.

'No.' Amy forced a smile. 'Just having five minutes' rest before I start.'

'We almost cancelled this particular clinic as it's the week between Christmas and New Year, but there were so many patients that in the end I decided that we had to run it. Are you going to eat that sandwich in front of you or just look at it?' Kate flicked the switch on the kettle and waited for it to boil.

'I'm not really hungry.' *It was a shame they hadn't cancelled the clinic.*

'You have a busy afternoon ahead of you. You should eat lunch.' Kate made her coffee and added some milk. 'Is it Marco that's made you lose your appetite? What's going on with the two of you?'

Amy hesitated. Kate was a friend, but she wasn't used to confiding in people. All her life she'd made her own decisions and relied on herself. To begin with she'd had no choice, and then it had become a way of life. 'We're— Well, let's just say our relationship is still over. We're just working a few things out.'

'That must be hard.' Kate put her mug on the table and sat down. 'You're very pale, Amy. Are you ill? Or is it just the stress of seeing Marco again?'

Could she pretend she was ill?

It would get her out of doing the clinic and it wasn't altogether a lie. The mere thought of spending an afternoon talking to pregnant women was enough to make her ill. But if she said she was ill, Marco would be on to her, trying to find out what was wrong.

'I'm not ill.'

'Then it must be stress. Do you honestly think the two of you are going to be able to work together?' Kate slowly stirred sugar into her coffee. 'I know that Nick's worried about it. He thinks that the history between you is going to make things difficult.'

'It will be fine. Nick has nothing to worry about. Marco and I are not planning to discuss the demise of our marriage at work.'

'No—all the same, it was good of you to stay and help us. I'm guessing that you didn't want to but Marco is very persuasive, as we both know. He has a way of getting a person to say yes to all sorts of things.' Kate's voice was gentle. 'Whatever you say to the contrary, I know this can't be easy for you, Amy. I never really understood what went wrong between the two of you but if you want someone to talk to, you have a friend in me. I just wanted to remind you of that.'

'Thanks. Thanks, Kate.' Unbelievably touched, Amy rose to her feet quickly before she was tempted to blurt out the truth about the current situation. 'Love is complicated, isn't it? And painful.' She had no doubt that Kate knew firsthand how painful love could be. Hadn't she lost her husband in a tragedy at sea that had left her to bring up a child alone?

'Yes. It's both those things.'

'How are things with you? How is Jeremiah?'

'Jem? He's fine. Really good. He's eight now. Unbelievable, really, how time passes.' For a moment, Kate stared blankly into the distance and then she cleared her throat and reached for her coffee, suddenly brisk and efficient. 'I envy you doing the antenatal clinic. At least pregnant women are healthy and cheerful.'

Amy's smile froze. 'Yes.'

'There are days when I miss midwifery.'

'I'd forgotten that you're a trained midwife.' *This was a conversation she didn't want to be having.* 'I'd better get on. I'll see you later, Kate.'

She had a clinic to run. A clinic that she didn't want to take. And she needed to prepare herself.

Amy worked on automatic, barely registering the identity of each patient.

It was as if a part of her mind was shut off.

By four o'clock, she only had one pregnant woman left to go and she poured herself a glass of water and drank deeply, promising herself that she was going to go straight home after the clinic. She was going to go straight home and hide under the duvet.

The door opened and her last patient walked in, a blonde woman in her late twenties, carrying a baby in a car seat.

'I know, I know, you're thinking I'm in the wrong clinic.' The woman laughed and sat down on the chair. 'Can you believe it? This little one is only four months old and I'm pregnant again! It's done wonders for my husband's ego. He thinks he's some sort of stallion. So much for the contraceptive effects of breastfeeding! I didn't believe it at first but I've done the test three times so I don't think there's any doubt. I rang for an appointment and they told me to come along this afternoon. They like you to get checked out as soon as possible these days, don't they?'

'That's right. You did the right thing to come.' Amy's mouth dried. 'Congratulations. Are you pleased?'

'Oh, yes. Well, Geoff, that's my husband, always wanted

a large family so it's not a problem. We hadn't quite planned on having them so close together but it's quite good when they're close in age, isn't it?' The baby started to cry and she bent down, undid the straps and gently lifted the baby from the car seat. 'Oh, now I've woken him up with my loud voice. Are you ready for your milk? Ridiculous, isn't it? Breastfeeding while you're pregnant. I mean, that's one of the things I wanted to talk to you about. Is it OK? I don't want to deprive the new baby of nutrients or anything.'

Amy watched as the woman lifted her jumper and skilfully attached the baby to her breast. The baby greedily clamped its jaws around her nipple and then closed his eyes and started to suck, a blissful expression on his face.

What did it feel like?

'Are you all right, Dr Avanti?' The woman frowned at her. 'You look a bit pale, yourself.'

'I'm fine,' Amy said tonelessly.

'And you're married to the other Dr Avanti. Lucky you. Now, that's a man any woman would want to make babies with.'

The pain inside her was so vicious that it took Amy a moment to find the breath to speak. 'It shouldn't be a problem to continue breastfeeding.' Somehow she forced herself to deliver the facts. 'Your biggest problem is likely to be that you'll feel very tired. Make sure you get plenty of rest and eat well. The taste of the milk might change and the baby might object to that for a while…' With difficulty she got through the consultation, saying what needed to be said and carrying out the tests that needed to be done.

By the time she finally closed the door on her consulting room at the end of clinic she felt emotionally drained. Sliding back into her chair, she felt the hot sting of tears behind her eyes.

Appalled at herself, she took a huge gulping breath and tried to control her emotions, but her misery was just too great to be contained and the tears spilled down her cheeks as the dam broke.

Sobs tore through her body and she put her head in her arms and gave in to it, crying like a child, consumed by the emotion that had been building inside her for so long.

She didn't hear the door open—wasn't aware of anything apart from her own misery until she felt a gentle hand on her shoulder and the sound of her name.

She gave a start and lifted her head to find Nick standing there, a look of concern on his face. 'Amy? What's happened?'

'Nothing.' Mortified, she sat up instantly and rubbed her palms over her cheeks, trying to compose herself. 'Well, this is embarrassing. I'm so sorry. *Really* sorry. I'm just tired or something. It's been a bit of a long week.' Her voice was thickened by crying and she knew that she must look a mess.

'Tired?' He studied her for a moment and then pulled up a chair and sat down next to her. 'No one cries like that just because they're tired. Are you depressed?'

Depressed?

Sodden with misery, Amy just stared at him. Clearly he wasn't going to leave her alone without an explanation and she was worn out with searching for new explanations that would keep people satisfied. 'Honestly, I'm not depressed. I'm sorry, Nick.' She yanked a tissue out of the box on her desk and blew her nose hard. 'That was very unprofessional of me. I can assure you that I was fine in front of the patients. I didn't—'

'Amy.' His tone was gruff as he interrupted her anxious apology. 'At this precise moment I don't give a damn about the patients. I'm not thinking about the patients. It's you that I'm worried about.'

'That's kind of you.' She blew her nose again and then gave him a smile. 'But there's no need to worry. I'm fine. Really.'

'Fine doesn't make you sob your heart out on the desk. Does this have something to do with the antenatal clinic? You really didn't want to run it, did you? And we didn't listen.'

'It's not the antenatal clinic.'

Nick watched her. 'Did you lose a baby, Amy?'

'No!' She shot him an anguished look, the pain twisting inside her. 'No, I didn't.'

'Then what's this about? Tell me.'

Amy teetered on the edge of confession and then suddenly remembered just who Nick was. 'I can't.' The tears threatened to start again and she gritted her teeth. 'I— It wouldn't be fair to you.'

'So it's something to do with your relationship with Marco and you're afraid that telling me would put me in a difficult position. You're also not sure that you trust me not to tell him. He mentioned that you'd changed your mind about having a family. Is this related?'

'Don't ask me. I can't talk to you, Nick.'

'I'm your doctor. You can talk to me and it's confidential.'

She blew her nose again and gave a watery smile. 'You're not my doctor. I've only been back in the country for five minutes. I don't have a doctor.'

'Well, you clearly need one, so from now on I'm officially your doctor. Kate will take care of the paperwork.' There was a faint trace of humour in his eyes. 'I need new patients. In case you hadn't noticed, we're nowhere near busy enough around here. I want to know why you were crying, Amy.'

She looked at him, her reluctance dissolving under the kindness she saw in his eyes. 'I find the antenatal clinic difficult.'

'Yes. I gathered that.' His voice was soft. 'Tell me why, Amy. Tell me why you find it difficult.'

She waited a heartbeat. 'Because I can't have children. I'm infertile.'

Nick was silent for a moment and then he sat back in his chair and gave a slow nod. 'All right. Now things are starting to make more sense. And this, presumably, is why you ended a relationship with a man you love?'

'I had no choice.'

'What about Marco? Didn't you think he deserved to know?'

'Don't judge me, Nick!' Her voice sharp, she rose to her feet and paced across the consulting room. Then she turned and wrapped her arms around her body, rubbing her hands up her arms to try and warm herself. 'I did what had to be done.'

'Can we take this a step at a time? When the two of you first arrived in Penhally, you were planning to start a family, I know. That's why you didn't bother finding a job. You were chasing around looking for suitable houses. You'd only been together for a few months. Given that you were in your early thirties, I wouldn't have expected you to become pregnant immediately. It often doesn't work like that, as you well know.'

'I know.' Should she tell him the truth? 'I went for tests.'

'After three months?'

'It was longer than that. By the time I had the tests, we'd been together for six months. No contraception. No pregnancy.' She started to pace again. 'To begin with I thought what you thought. I said all those things women always say to themselves when they're trying to get pregnant. Six months is nothing. I'm over thirty, it might take a while. And then I bumped into an old friend I was in med school with and she turned out to be an infertility specialist at a clinic in Exeter. I decided I may as well have some tests.'

'You didn't tell Marco?'

'No.' She stopped pacing. 'I wanted to find out for myself.'

'So what did the tests show?'

'Scarring.' Such a simple word for something that had had such a massive impact on her life. 'Mild endometriosis. Not enough to need treatment but quite enough to interfere with my fertility. The doctor said that my Fallopian tubes are completely gummed up.'

Nick listened carefully and then he stirred. 'Well, the first thing to say is that infertility is a particularly inexact science. No doctor would ever be able to be one hundred per cent sure that you were infertile.'

'She said that if an egg ever made it along my Fallopian tube, she'd be surprised.'

'Well, we've just had snow in Cornwall.' He gave a wry smile. 'So life is full of surprises, Amy.'

'I know that miracles happen. I know all that, Nick.' She was touched by his kindness. Often with his colleagues Nick was brusque and sometimes even sharp-tongued. But there was no doubting his concern for her at that moment. 'But I couldn't risk our marriage and Marco's happiness on a hope. The chances are that I will never be able to get pregnant.'

'And that was enough for you to decide to end your marriage?'

'It was enough for me.' *More than enough.*

'Let's assume for the sake of argument that your Fallopian tubes are blocked—there are still other options. IVF? Adoption?'

Amy stilled. 'Those aren't options for me.'

'Why not?'

'I have my reasons.' And she wasn't going to share those reasons with anyone. She'd already said more than enough. 'So now you see why I had to leave.'

'Well, not really, no. I see why you *think* you had to leave. You managed to convince yourself that Marco would be better off without you. So you spun a story about choosing a career over a family and about not loving him enough.'

'I had to give him a reason.'

'Why not give him the truth?'

'Because then he would have felt an obligation towards me. I was already his wife. I decided that the easiest way was just to end the relationship. It would have ended at some point anyway, so I didn't do anything except bring forward the inevitable.'

'That's a very negative attitude. Why would it have ended anyway?'

'Because infertility wrecks marriages. It tears them apart.' She stared out of the window, her expression bleak. 'Even strong marriages, and ours wasn't that strong. We hadn't known each other long. He didn't love me enough.'

'Didn't he? That's interesting,' Nick said calmly. 'So why did he go completely off the rails when you left?'

Startled, Amy turned to him. 'What do you mean, "off the rails"?'

'I'll spare you the details but let's just say that he wasn't a happy man.' Nick's eyes narrowed. 'I've known Marco for years, as you know. I can honestly say that you were the first woman he ever really loved.'

'He didn't love me. He couldn't have done.'

'Why not?'

'Because we were together such a short time.'

'But you loved him in that same short time,' Nick pointed out calmly, and she gave a reluctant nod.

'Yes, but…he didn't love me.' Amy frowned and shook her head. 'He never said.'

'Ah. Didn't he?' Nick gave a wry smile. 'Well, we men are terrible at saying what women want to hear, you should know that. But just because the words aren't there doesn't mean that the emotions aren't.'

'He didn't love me, Nick.' She clasped her hands in front of her. 'He didn't try and stop me going.'

'He was in shock. You'd just bought a house to move into together and then suddenly you changed overnight. He assumed you'd met someone else and were just throwing excuses at him.'

Amy felt the colour drain from her face. 'There was no one else. There's never been anyone else.'

'I'm just telling you what he assumed. He couldn't think of anything else that would explain the sudden shift in your behaviour.'

'Is that why he didn't come after me?'

'He's a proud man, Amy. He assumed that you wanted to get away from him so he wasn't about to follow you. And after he calmed down—well, that was when things fell apart here.' Nick's face was expressionless as he referred obliquely to the death of his wife. 'I expect he felt he couldn't leave.'

'Of course he couldn't. I understand. It must have been a horrendous time for you. And I didn't want, or expect, Marco to follow me.' She closed her eyes for a moment. 'I'm so, so sorry about your wife, Nick.'

'We're talking about you, not me.'

'I think we've said all there is to say. I can't have a child, Nick. I can't give Marco the family he wants so badly. And he *does* want it badly—you of all people should know that. He's Italian. He wants a big, noisy, busy family with at least four children as beautiful as he is, fighting over the large bowl of spaghetti in the middle of the table.'

'I don't understand why you're so black and white about this.' Nick stood up and rubbed his forehead with the tips of his fingers. 'There are other options, Amy. If it's so important to you both, you could look for a solution.'

The past clawed at her and she gave a little shake of her head, trying to dispel the memories. *It was always there in the background.*

'I'm not interested in any of those options. I've seen

what—' She broke off but Nick's questioning gaze was enough to tell her that she'd already said too much.

'What have you seen, Amy?'

'Nothing.' Her voice was hoarse. 'Nothing. I just know that those aren't options.'

Nick studied her face for a moment but he didn't push her for more information. 'Well, at least now I understand why you didn't want to do the antenatal clinic.'

'It was difficult,' she said honestly, 'but you don't come to terms with something by ignoring it, so I'm sure that taking that clinic will do me good in the long term.'

'Some things are more difficult to come to terms with than others. Marco can do that clinic from now on, Amy. Or I will. You can do child health or minor surgery.'

'If we swap things around then he'll ask questions that I don't want to answer, and anyway he should do child health—he's a paediatrician. I'll be fine, Nick. I can do the clinic.' Amy walked back to her desk and picked up her coat and bag. 'I'm sorry to dump all over you like this. I can't think what came over me.'

'If a problem is big enough then it eventually finds its way out,' Nick said softly, and Amy slipped on her wool coat and belted it.

'Maybe.'

'My guess is that you've bottled this up for two years. You should talk to someone about it. Talking can help.'

She picked up her bag. 'Do you talk to anyone, Nick?'

His gaze held hers for a moment and then he gave a humourless laugh. 'I'm not sure if you win that point or not. It's different. I'm a man.'

'And you know as well as I do that talking doesn't always help anything. Sometimes it makes things worse. I'd be grateful if you didn't say anything to Marco.'

'He'd want to know, Amy.'

'It would make everything a thousand times more compli-cated and painful and it wouldn't change the outcome.'

'He loves you.'

Amy felt as though her heart was being squeezed by a vice. 'Even if that were true, it wouldn't change the outcome either,' she said quietly, walking towards the door. 'Thanks, Nick, for listening. Actually, it *was* good to tell someone. I feel better now. More in control. I can do this. I can work as a locum and then walk away and pursue a career.'

'And is that what you want?'

She paused with her hand on the door. 'No. But life doesn't always give you what you want, does it?'

'No. It doesn't.'

She left the room and immediately bumped into Marco in the corridor. Knowing that the evidence of her distress would still show on her face, she kept walking. 'I've finished the clinic. I'll see you at home.' She kept her head down but he caught her arm.

'You're always in such a hurry! I just spoke to the hospital. Eddie doesn't have a skull fracture and they're happy with him. He's coming home tomorrow.'

'That's good. Really good. His mother must be relieved.' She glanced at her watch. 'I've got to dash.'

'Why?' He slid a hand under her chin, lifted her face and then swore softly. 'You've been crying.'

'No, of course I haven't.' She tried to ease her arm away from his grip but he held her firmly.

'Your eyes are red.'

'I think I'm getting a cold.' She sniffed to prove the point. 'It's that time of year. Germs everywhere.'

'Germs don't give you swollen eyes. You've been crying, Amy. Why?'

Given the determined pressure of his fingers, she had no choice but to look into his eyes and this time there was no trace of anger. Just concern. And the concern brought the lump back to her throat.

Oh, for goodness' sake, what was the matter with her? Why did her body have to pick this particular moment to release all the tension that had been building inside her? She'd had two years to break down and she'd chosen the most inappropriate moment possible and the most public place.

With a determined effort she freed herself from his grasp and stepped away from him. 'Honestly, I'm fine. I'm really, really pleased about little Eddie. I'll see you at home.' And she turned and hurried away from him.

CHAPTER SEVEN

'SHE was crying.' Marco followed Nick back into his consulting room, anger shaking his powerful frame. 'Amy has been crying and you were with her! What did you say to her?'

'I can't discuss it.'

'You *will* discuss it!' Marco slammed the door shut with the flat of his hand and gave a low growl. 'This is my wife we're talking about.'

'You're separated.'

'She's *my wife.*'

'Why would you care if she's upset?' Nick's tone was even. 'You've been angry enough with her for the past two years.'

'She left me. I'm human. Yes, I was angry. But that doesn't stop me caring about her.'

Nick sat down in his chair. 'How much do you care about her?'

'What sort of a question is that? So now you are—what do they call it?' His English momentarily abandoning him, Marco switched to Italian and then back again. 'A marriage counsellor?'

'Do you still love her?'

Thrown by the intimacy of the question, Marco prowled across the consulting room and stared blankly at the wall displaying a poster on the dangers of smoking. 'Yes. I still love her.' He turned sharply. 'So now will you tell me why she was crying?'

'I can't do that. Our talk was confidential.'

'So you *do* know what's wrong.' Exasperated, Marco spread his hands in question. 'Tell me what she said! How could it be confidential?'

'Because she spoke to me as a doctor.'

'It was a consultation?'

'Yes.'

'She's ill?' Anxiety replaced anger, but the emotion was just as sharp. 'Is something the matter with her?' He'd wondered. It might explain why she'd lost weight and why she was looking so pale.

'She isn't ill.'

Marco let out a long breath. For a moment he'd been afraid that— 'Well, if she wasn't ill, why did she need to talk to a doctor?'

Nick was silent for a moment. 'How well do you know Amy?'

Marco frowned and rubbed a hand over his face. 'Well enough to love her. I know the sort of person she is. She's shy with people she doesn't know, she finds it quite hard to talk about her feelings but underneath she's very loving and giving. She loves children, or at least I always thought she did.' Marco broke off, wondering why he was revealing so much to his partner. 'I don't understand what you're getting at.'

'How much do you know about her past? Her background? Before she met you?'

'I don't know. Not much. I never really worried about it. It's not that relevant, is it?' His gaze sharpened. 'You think it's relevant?'

'I don't know.' Nick's voice was thoughtful. 'I think it

could be. If you want my advice, and frankly I wouldn't blame you if you didn't take it because advice on the matters of the heart isn't exactly my strong suit, I'd get to know her better. I mean the Amy underneath. What makes her tick? What made her believe the things she believes? Find that out and you might find the answers you're looking for.'

'You can't tell me more than that?'

'No. I can't.' Nick leaned forward and switched on his computer. 'That's already far more than I should have said.'

Amy took a hot shower but it didn't stop the shivering. Desperate for warmth, she dressed in a pair of jeans and a warm jumper, her hair hanging damp and loose to her shoulders.

Her head throbbed from crying and outside the wind had picked up. The sky was grey and threatening and the word among the villagers was that there was more snow on the way.

Still shivering, she walked down to the kitchen to make herself a hot drink. The conversation with Nick had left her feeling raw and vulnerable. She felt slightly odd, having exposed so much of herself to another person. And yet, despite that, telling Nick had made her feel better. He was the first person she'd confided in and she felt lighter.

Or did she feel lighter because he'd told her that Marco had been so badly affected by her departure?

He'd cared.

And she'd so badly wanted him to care. Not that it changed anything, she reminded herself miserably. It didn't change anything at all. No relationship was strong enough to withstand such a bitter blow—she knew that better than anyone.

Thoughts flew into her head and clashed, a cacophony of childhood memories that unsettled and disturbed her.

Not now. *She wasn't going to think about any of that now.*

Hearing the unmistakable sound of the Maserati, Amy tensed.

Marco was home.

Which meant more questions.

She was just debating whether to go up to the spare room and close the door when she heard his key in the door and moments later he walked into the kitchen.

'It's freezing out there and as for the wind…' He gave a shudder that more eloquently described his views on the weather than his words did. 'They were planning fireworks on New Year's Eve but they won't be able to do them if this wind keeps up. It will be too dangerous. We will be treating burn victims.'

Amy found herself looking at the curve of his mouth and then at the dark shadow of stubble on his hard jaw. She turned away quickly. 'It will be a shame if we have to cancel. The fireworks are always a highlight of New Year in Penhally. I used to love them when I was a child.' *Why did she still have to feel like this?* It was so unfair!

Marco reached for a bottle of wine. 'You stayed with your grandmother?'

'That's right.'

'In the cottage? I've often wondered why you sold it.'

'It would have been too small for us.'

'*Sì*, but I would have thought it had sentimental value.' He jerked the cork out of the bottle and reached for a glass. 'Wine?'

'No, thanks.'

'You look tired.' His eyes lingered on hers for a moment and then he turned away and poured wine into his own glass.

Her heart pumping hard, Amy closed her eyes briefly, hoping that he couldn't sense her body's response to him. Everything suddenly felt confused. She'd arrived with one clear objective and an iron resolve, but now everything was clouded. Suddenly what she had to do and what she wanted to do seemed a million miles apart.

It was just because she was living and working with him, she thought helplessly. Marco didn't exactly melt into the background. He was a very confident, very physical man. Even now, with his powerful shoulders and long, strong legs, he seemed to fill the room, and suddenly the large, beautiful kitchen seemed claustrophobically small.

'So, your grandmother's house—was it full of memories?'

Full of memories, many of them not good. 'I didn't want to keep it.' Why was he watching her so closely? *Had Nick said something to him?*

'You're very tense,' he said softly. 'Is something wrong?'

Of course she was tense. She was so aware of him that it was almost impossible to breathe.

'Amy?' He stepped towards her and lifted a hand, stroking her hair away from her forehead with the tips of his fingers. 'Do you have a headache?'

This was insane. She had to move away now. The brush of his fingers set her body on fire, even though she knew that his touch hadn't been sexual in nature.

Her gaze lifted to his and she saw the hot burn in his eyes, the look they exchanged an intimate meshing of their thoughts.

Terrified that he'd see too much, Amy moved away from him, ignoring the instinct that was telling her to move closer. 'I do have a slight headache. Do you have any paracetamol in the house?'

His eyes didn't leave hers. 'Go and lie on the sofa. I'll bring you something.'

Relieved to put some space between them, she did as he suggested and moments later he reappeared with a glass of water and the tablets.

'Thank you.' She took them gratefully and then leaned her aching head against the back of the sofa, hoping that the tablets wouldn't take long to work. 'Sorry. Long day.'

'I can imagine.' He took the water from her, put it on the table and then moved behind the sofa.

The next thing she felt was the touch of his hands in her hair. 'Marco—'

'This will ease the pain of your headache far more effectively than medication,' he murmured softly, sliding his fingers into her hair and gently massaging her scalp. 'I remember that you often had headaches when we first met.'

'Like little Harry. Poor thing. I wouldn't wish this on anyone.' She knew she ought to move but she couldn't. His fingers were firm and rhythmic as they moved over her scalp. 'That feels good.'

'Tell me about the Penhally fireworks. Tell me about your grandmother.' His voice was deep and soothing and her eyes drifted shut.

'I stayed with my grandmother every Christmas and New Year, right through the holidays. There was a window-seat in my bedroom and on New Year's Eve I'd kneel there and watch the fireworks—they were fantastic. Then we'd have hot chocolate together. When I was older, I was allowed to go along and watch.'

'And that was fun?'

'Yes. Everyone was very friendly.' For a short time she'd felt as though she'd belonged somewhere.

'You spent every holiday with your grandmother?'

'Because my mother was working right through and she couldn't look after me.'

'And your father?'

The question disturbed the calm flow of her thoughts. 'My father spent every Christmas with his twenty-four-year-old secretary.'

'Ah...' Marco's fingers stopped moving. 'He had an affair?'

'It started as an affair, but then he married her and at the last count they had four beautiful children, two boys and two girls.' The tension flowed back into her veins and she sat up. 'Why are we talking about my father?'

'Why not?' He walked over to the table and picked up his wine. 'You said that we didn't know each other well enough and I'm starting to think that perhaps you were right. I want to know more about your life before I met you. It must have been tough, spending every holiday with your grandmother.'

'I loved it,' she said honestly. 'She was a wonderful woman.'

'You didn't miss your home? Your mother?'

Her heart beating rapidly, Amy rose to her feet. 'No, not really. What is this? The Spanish Inquisition?'

'*Calmo, tesoro.*' His voice was soft. 'Suddenly your voice is rising and you're very tense. Why does a simple question feel like an inquisition? Is the subject matter that painful?'

'Painful? I didn't say it was painful,' she said quickly. 'I just don't see how my past is in any way relevant to our current situation. You don't *need* to know any more about me, Marco. It's irrelevant. Our marriage is over, we both know that.' She regretted the words instantly, knowing that such a declaration simply invited the very response on his part that she was trying to avoid.

'It is over? Ah, yes.' His tone was deceptively casual as he strolled across the room towards her. 'I remember now. It is over because you feel nothing for me, isn't that right?'

She didn't dare look at him and she didn't need to because his slightly husky, lazy drawl revealed his feelings all too clearly. Amy ceased to breathe. 'I think I'll go upstairs and—'

'You're not going anywhere.' Without allowing her time to move, he curved an arm around her waist in an unmis- takably possessive gesture and pulled her against him, ignoring her soft gasp of protest.

'What are you doing?'

'What I should have done two years ago. When you talk, nothing makes sense so the obvious solution is to try a different method of communication.' She was breathlessly aware of the dangerous glint in his eyes and then his mouth came down on hers and they were kissing, their mouths hungry, the pleasure hot and instantaneous.

It was like a storm breaking and Amy sank her fingers into the hard muscle of his shoulders to stop herself sliding to the floor. Her legs shook, her whole body trembled and the heat of his mouth coaxed a response from her, even though she was dimly aware that what they were doing now was going to make everything much more complicated later.

She didn't care about later. She only cared about *now*, and anyway it was impossible to think or concentrate when his skilful hands were reacquainting themselves with her body. They slid under her jumper and stroked the warm skin of her back and then they moved back to her waist and one thumb circled her navel. And all the time he kissed her, his mouth and hands creating sensations that threatened to consume her.

She'd missed him so much.

The hot, desperate kiss was briefly interrupted as he pulled her jumper over her head and then her shirt followed and her bra until she stood only in her jeans, shaking and shivering in his arms.

'You are cold?' He muttered the question against her mouth and she shook her head, wondering how she was expected to answer when she could barely stand.

'No. Not cold.'

Hot. *Dangerously, deliciously hot.*

Marco kissed her again and she clung to him as he pulled her gently off balance and lowered her onto the thick rug. Next to them the fire flickered but neither of them noticed or cared.

Amy could hardly breathe and she gave a low moan as his

mouth moved to her breast, his tongue teasing her nipple to hardness. He seduced and tormented until the sensation that shot through her body was almost agonising in its intensity. And then he shifted his attention to her other breast and Amy writhed and gasped, her body arching against his as he used all his skill and experience to drag a response from her.

Oblivious to everything except her own need for him, she reached down to touch him and only then realised that he was still fully clothed. With a whimper of frustration she tugged at the belt of his trousers and he covered her hand with his and swiftly helped her.

Amy felt her mouth dry as Marco dragged off his own clothes, revealing a body that was hard and fit. Had she really thought she'd ever be indifferent to this man? He had an amazing physique, the muscles of his shoulders and arms curved, his stomach flat and the movement of his body fluid.

Then he turned back to her and lowered his head, his mouth hot and hard and the touch of his fingers skilled and impossibly intimate. He wasn't slow or gentle but she didn't care because this wasn't about seduction—it was about wild, desperate need. And when he finally parted her thighs she gave a whimper of assent and wrapped her legs around him. Nothing mattered any more. Nothing except this. *Nothing except him.*

She felt the thickness of his arousal and then he paused for a moment and looked straight into her eyes, strands of inky black hair falling over his forehead, his breathing uneven. 'Amy?'

'Don't stop, Marco.' She virtually sobbed the words, her hands sliding over his warm skin, urging him forward. 'Please…'

He hesitated for just a moment and then moved his hips and entered her in a single, smooth thrust that joined them completely.

It had been so long.

The sudden intimacy overwhelmed her and then he started to move and each powerful stroke felt shockingly delicious. All she was aware of was him, the intoxicating scent of him, the skilled touch of his fingers, *the hard male pulse of his body*. He didn't take it slowly and she didn't care. Frantic, desperate, she urged him faster and he drove his body into hers with ruthless, reckless hunger until the tingle and burn inside her grew into something that couldn't be contained and her body exploded.

Her climax was shockingly intense and she heard his harsh groan and knew that her body had driven through his control and tipped him over the edge. He exploded inside her and her fingers dug hard into the slick muscle of his shoulders, clinging as they rode the storm, oblivious to everything around them.

Eventually the wildness eased and they lay for a moment, their bodies still joined and their minds still numb.

And then Marco rolled onto his back, drawing her against him. 'That was incredible. *You* are incredible.'

Amy closed her eyes tightly, waiting for the aftershocks to pass.

What had they done? What had *she* done?

For a moment she lay there, her body still weak and drugged from the after-effects of his love-making. 'We shouldn't have done that.'

'Why not? We're still married, *tesoro*. Sex is part of a relationship.'

'We don't have a relationship, Marco, not any more.' More than a little confused, she sat up and immediately felt the hot burn of his gaze on her body. Horribly self-conscious, she reached for her jumper and pulled it over her head. 'Nothing has changed.'

It took him a moment to answer and he rubbed a hand over his face, as if forcing himself to concentrate. 'You can't truly

believe that.' His voice was soft and when he finally looked
at her, his gaze was dark. '*Everything* has changed, *amore*.'

'No, it hasn't.' She reached for her jeans and wriggled into
them. 'I— The sex was great, Marco, you know that. But it
doesn't change the fact that we no longer have a relationship.'

He lifted a brow in silent mockery. 'A moment ago, when I
was inside you, did that not feel as though we had a relationship?'

She felt her face turn scarlet. 'Don't talk like that.'

He gave a soft laugh. 'How can you still be shy with me?
You are the most complex, confusing woman I've ever met.
You don't mind indulging in hot, mindless sex but you don't
want to talk about it. Don't pretend that nothing has changed
between us, Amy. That would be foolish. And a waste of
time. I'm not stupid and neither are you.'

She rose to her feet, unable to resist a sideways glance at
his naked body. He was magnificent—his body lean and
muscular, his stomach taut and flat, his olive skin liberally
dusted with a pattern of dark hair that emphasised his virility
and masculinity.

'Marco, don't do this. Please, don't do this.'

He rose to his feet, completely unselfconscious. 'You've
lost weight.' Ignoring her plea, he slid a hand around her
waist and drew her against him. 'But you're still beautiful.'

Amy put a hand on his chest. 'No.'

'Yes,' Marco purred softly, sliding his hands inside her
jumper and smoothing her spine. 'Let's go upstairs to bed.
This time we take more time. *Lentamente. Gentilmente.*'

Slow. Gentle.

Amy felt the smooth masculine tones connect with her
insides. 'That would just confuse things even more and I'm
confused enough already.'

'I am not at all confused.' He brushed her hair away from
her neck, lowered his head and delivered a lingering kiss to

the base of her throat. 'I am entirely clear about everything. And now we have the whole weekend ahead of us to make up for lost time.'

'No!' Dizzy from his touch, Amy gave him a push and forced herself to step backwards. 'No, Marco! I meant what I said—nothing has changed. You're not listening to me! I'm talking and you're *just not listening*!' Not trusting herself to be so close to him and not touch him, she walked over to the window and stared out into the darkness. Beyond the glass came the faint sound of the sea crashing onto the rocks below the house. 'All right, so we had sex—good sex—but it doesn't change the facts. We want different things. You still want a family and I still want a career.'

'Ah, yes.' He sounded unperturbed. 'A career. You don't love me enough, isn't that right?'

'That's right.' After what they'd just shared, she couldn't look at him. 'I don't.'

'And you always have sex with men that you have no feeling for, no? That is so typical of you, isn't it, *tesoro*?'

How did he know so much about her when they'd spent so little time together? She forced herself to turn, noticing in a glance that he'd pulled on his trousers but his torso was still bare. 'I can understand why you might read more into what just happened but, please, don't. It really was just sex, Marco. And it wasn't that surprising. The chemistry between us always led us into trouble.'

His gaze was brooding. 'Talking of trouble—since you are still so set on following this career path and not having a family, we probably ought to talk about contraception.'

'There's no need. It won't happen again.'

'I wasn't talking about the future,' he said gently, reaching for his jumper, 'I was talking about the past. We just had unprotected sex, *amore*. Do you want the morning-after pill? I have some in my bag.'

She froze. 'No.' Her mouth was so dry she could barely answer the question. 'No, that won't be necessary.'

'Why not?' He moved towards her, his eyes intent on her face. 'You have decided that you will take your chances? If you become pregnant, you will have a family and abandon your ideas of a career? You are leaving the choice to fate perhaps?'

'None of those things. There just isn't any way I could get pregnant.' She kept her tone casual, assuming that he'd take her comment to mean that it was the wrong time of the month, but he swore softly in Italian and his eyes darkened with anger.

Amy watched him, confused by his reaction. Only a moment ago he'd offered her contraception. Surely he wouldn't want her to get pregnant, given the mess that their marriage was in?

So why did he look as though he wanted to put his fist through the window?

Marco ran out of the back door and onto the coast road. It was dark but he didn't care because he knew the road as well as he knew his own kitchen and he needed to burn off his anger.

She'd turned down the morning-after pill.

There was no way she could get pregnant. Wasn't that what she'd said?

So what did that mean? That she was already taking contraception?

They'd been apart for two years so there was only one reason why she would be using contraception.

Jealousy dug its claws in deep and he increased his speed, pounding along the road, ignoring the punch of the wind and the bite of the cold as he tried to outrun his demons.

Obviously it was as he'd first suspected.

She'd found someone else.

Was that why she'd been crying? Was that why Nick had encouraged him to find out more about her past? Was this man an ex-lover? Someone she'd known before she'd met him?

Marco pounded along the road, his mind full of questions.

Was this mystery man the reason she'd been so intent on ending their marriage?

He ran until the breath tore through his lungs and then he stopped, breathing heavily, forcing his mind to work.

This was Amy. *Amy.* Not any other woman. She wasn't a woman to take a string of lovers. Despite the evidence, it didn't fit with what he knew of her.

Amy would only indulge in a physical relationship with a man if she cared deeply.

But if she didn't have another man, why was she using contraception?

Marco ran a hand over the back of his neck, remembering the way she'd clung to him and urged him on, *remembering the sort of woman he knew her to be*, and knew that he wasn't mistaken in her feelings for him.

She cared deeply. For him. After what they'd shared that afternoon, he knew that she was still in love with him. So why was she so intent on denying it?

Why did she want to end their marriage?

Amy lay on the bed with her eyes wide open, staring at the ceiling, full of regrets. She should have kept her distance from Marco. She should have known that she wouldn't be able to resist him.

If only she'd walked away from him the moment she'd felt the tension sizzling between them.

If only she had more self-control.

If only—the two most useless words in the human language. The slam of the door downstairs announced that Marco was back from his run, but judging from the violence of the sound his temper hadn't improved.

Hardly surprising perhaps, running in the freezing wind in the darkness.

Amy closed her eyes, feeling nothing but sympathy for him. Their impulsive love-making session had left her feeling equally confused and frustrated. That was what happened when you gave in to chemistry.

It produced complications.

It was some consolation that he had no more self-control than she did.

The door to her bedroom opened and she turned her head and saw him standing in the doorway, broad-shouldered and powerful. There was a sheen of sweat on his forehead and he'd clearly pushed himself to the limit physically.

His eyes glittered darkly and his mouth was set in a grim line. 'Is there someone else?'

'I'm sorry?' The question was so surprising that she sat up instantly, her eyes wide. 'What do you mean, someone else?'

'It's a plausible reason for you to end our marriage.'

'Marco, I've told you why I ended our marriage. There isn't anyone else in my life.' And there never would be. She had nothing to offer any man.

'So why are you taking contraception?'

'I never said that I was—' She broke off, realising too late that she'd revealed far too much yet again. How did people ever lie and cheat? She was hopeless, absolutely hopeless.

'You said that there was absolutely no chance that you could possibly become pregnant.'

Her heart pounded against her chest. 'It's just not the right time of the month.'

'Nature isn't that predictable, as you and I both know. If you are truly this career person now, why would you want to risk having a baby?' He strode into the room, his eyes fixed on her face. 'I've been thinking about this, going through the facts, sifting through the options, and I've only come up with one possible explanation for the way you're behaving. You don't think you *can* become pregnant, is that right?'

She felt the colour drain from her face. 'Marco...'

He watched her and nodded slowly. 'That's it, isn't it? You can't have a baby.'

Amy shrank back on the bed, her arms around her knees like a child. 'Go away, Marco.' She was shivering again and the headache was back. 'I want to be on my own.'

'Well, that's tough, because when you're married there are two people involved.' His voice soft, he sat down on the edge of the bed. 'An honest woman makes a hopeless liar, Amy, and you are an honest woman. Since the day you told me you were leaving, nothing you have said has made sense.'

'Marco, please—'

'You are a mass of inconsistencies. You keep telling me that you want a career and although you are undoubtedly an excellent doctor, it's always been clear to me that what you really long for is a family. You say you don't want children and yet I see you with them and you are warm and kind. And you say that you don't love me but when we are together...' he reached out and slid a hand under her jaw, gently insisting that she look at him '...you give everything, *tesoro*. What we shared earlier—that wasn't sex, it was love.'

She sucked in a juddering breath. 'Don't do this. The truth is that none of the reasons matter. The end is the same. I can't be with you.'

His thumb gently stroked her jaw. 'We both know that is nonsense. We were meant to be together.'

'No.' Tears welled up and spilled onto her cheeks. 'Don't let's have this conversation! I've already cried more today than in my whole life!'

'Emotion is a good thing. Only the English treat emotion

as if it were a dangerous animal.' His faintly humourous analysis of her countrymen would have made her smile at any other time.

But she was a long way from smiling.

She wiped one cheek with the back of her hand. 'Emotion gives you a headache.'

'*Cucciola mia.*'

She sniffed and tried to ignore the insistent brush of his fingers on her face. 'That's what you called Michelle. I don't even know what it means.'

'Literally?' He slid his hand behind her neck, leaned forward and kissed her gently on the mouth. Then he lifted his head and gave a slow smile. 'It is a puppy.'

'So now you're calling me a dog?'

He laughed softly. 'So now I finally see the Amy I used to know. For a long time she was afraid to come out, but I knew she was tucked away in there somewhere. I want to ask you something and I want an honest answer—probably the first one you've given me for a long time.'

'I don't want to talk about this.'

'Shh…' Amusement in his eyes, he pressed his fingers to her lips. 'You need to stop arguing with me. It's bad for you, *amore*, and it gives me indigestion. A good Italian wife should agree with everything her husband says.'

Her heart aching, she gave a wobbly smile. 'I don't think I'm a good Italian wife, that's what I've been trying to tell you.' Her smile faded. 'I can't do any of the things that a good Italian wife is supposed to do. For a start, I don't even speak the language.'

'This could be good! Most Italian men would kill to have a wife who couldn't answer back!' His eyes gleamed but this time she didn't manage a smile in response. How could he be so good about it all? Did he understand what she was telling him?

'You're refusing to take me seriously.'

'*Sì*, that's right, I am.' Suddenly his voice was deadly serious. 'Because you are talking nonsense. What is this about? Who is this "good Italian wife"? I didn't pick an Italian for my wife—I picked you.'

It was time to spell it out. 'But I can't have children, Marco. You're right about that. I'm infertile.' There. She'd said it. Finally, after two long years of anguish and misery, she'd said it. Such a small word for something so big.

There was a moment of silence and she saw a muscle flicker in his lean cheek but when he spoke his voice was calm and even. 'I understand that. What I *don't* understand is why this made you leave. Why would this have an impact on our marriage? Why didn't you share it with me?'

'Because I was afraid you'd say that it wouldn't make a difference.' She pulled away from him and hugged her knees tighter.

'It doesn't make a difference. A relationship starts with two people, *amore*. Later on more may be added but always it starts just with two.'

'I know how much you want children.'

'Look at me, Amy.' His voice was firm and he nodded when she lifted her head. 'That's better. Yes, I would like children but I am not a child myself. I know that life doesn't always give us what we want or plan for and being an adult is about making choices. When I asked you to marry me I made a choice, *tesoro*. You were my choice.'

She struggled with the tears again. 'Pretty lousy choice.'

'Certainly it's true I would have preferred to have a wife who didn't run away to a different continent for two years,' he said mildly, 'but you are back now and everything is sorted. That's all that matters.'

'How can you say that? Nothing is sorted.'

'*Belissima...*' His voice infinitely gentle, he cupped her

face in his hands and forced her to look at him. 'You are de-termined to make life so complicated.'

'You can't pretend that this is nothing, Marco!'

'No, I'm not going to do that. But neither am I going to sacrifice our relationship for it. And neither should you isolate yourself.' He said something in Italian and she looked at him expectantly.

'In English?'

He slid his fingers through her hair in an unmistakable gesture of affection. 'I said that this didn't happen to you, it happened to us. And now we will deal with it. There are lots of options.'

Unable to help herself, Amy leaned against his chest and felt his arms close around her. She felt his warmth, his strength and she closed her eyes for a moment, greedy for the comfort even though she knew it could only be temporary.

For her there were no options. None.

Marco locked the bathroom door securely and then crossed to the washbasin, his breathing unsteady as he struggled with the emotion that he'd been holding back.

Two years.

They'd wasted two years.

His jaw tensed and he gripped the edge of the basin so hard that his knuckles whitened.

When he'd finally realised the truth, it had taken all his self-control not to erupt with anger. But then he'd seen the torment in her eyes and realised that she'd made the decision to leave him based on a set of beliefs of which he had abso-lutely no understanding.

Was that what Nick had meant when he'd hinted that he should find out more about her past?

And what exactly was it in her past that made Amy so sure that their marriage couldn't survive the blow of infertility? Why did she think there were no options?

Inhaling deeply, Marco turned on the taps and splashed his face with cold water.

'Marco?' Amy's voice came from outside the bathroom, tentative and unsure. 'Are you all right?'

Marco reached for a towel and stared at his reflection in the mirror. *Was he all right?* He was angry, frustrated and disappointed, but he knew that displaying those emotions wouldn't help his cause.

What he needed to do was prove to Amy that their marriage had a future. And to do that he needed to understand why she was of the opposite opinion.

And she didn't need his anger. She needed his patience.

'I'm fine.' He kept his voice even. 'I'll be out in a moment, *amore*.'

And they were going to do some talking.

CHAPTER EIGHT

THE following morning Marco was no closer to answers despite having spent a long and sleepless night examining that question in detail.

He'd *known* she wasn't a career woman.

He'd *known* she'd loved him.

Why hadn't he managed to unravel the problem sooner?

Since when had he been so obtuse?

All he had to do now was convince her that it didn't make a difference to their marriage.

He heard a noise behind him and turned to find her standing in the doorway to the bathroom. She'd borrowed one of his T-shirts to sleep in and she looked impossibly young and slender, her face free of make-up and worryingly pale.

'*Buongiorno, tesoro.* I'm sorry if I woke you. I have surgery this morning.'

'So do I. I agreed it with Nick.' Her eyes slid from his and she gave an awkward smile. 'I'll go and use the other bathroom, shall I?'

'Go back to bed.' He splashed his face and reached for a towel. 'You're not in a fit state to do surgery. Yesterday was a huge trauma for you and you've had no sleep. I'll take your patients and I'll explain to Nick.'

'I'll be fine when I've had a shower.' After a moment's

hesitation she reached into the shower cubicle and turned on the water. 'You're not doing the surgery on your own, Dr Avanti. Who do you think you are? Superman?'

'Superdoctor, actually.' He watched hungrily as she pulled the T-shirt over her head and stepped naked into the shower. Her breasts were high and firm, her waist tiny and her hips gently curved. Gripped by a vicious attack of lust, Marco stood for a moment, feeling himself grow hard. Then he gave a soft curse and stepped into the shower with her.

She gave a gasp of shock and turned, clearing the water from her eyes. 'What are you doing? You've had your shower.'

'I decided I needed another one.' He stroked a hand down her smooth, silky skin and gave a groan of masculine appreciation. 'I've been deprived of your body for too long.'

'I thought you said I was too thin.'

He smiled and curved her body against his, ignoring the relentless sting of the water. 'My beautiful Amy, so much a woman. Always insecure and with no reason.'

'Marco…' She sounded breathless. 'We don't have time for this.'

'I can always make time for something important.'

'Things are complicated enough already—'

'If life isn't complicated, I become bored.' He buried his head in her neck and slid his hands over the soft curve of her bottom. Then he gave up on English and spoke only Italian.

'Marco, no…' But her words were insincere and her head fell back and her eyes closed. 'We really can't—*non posso*—' Then she gasped as she felt the intimate stroke of his fingers.

'You have been learning Italian for me?'

'Marco…' She stroked a hand over her face to remove the water. Her hair was dark and sleek under the jet of the shower, her eyelashes spiky. *And she'd never looked more beautiful.*

Unable to hold himself back a moment longer, Marco

brought his mouth down on hers. He felt her arms come round his neck, felt the tantalising brush of her firm breasts against his chest hair, and then he was pressing her back against the wall of the shower, his need for her so great that it bordered on the primitive.

With no preliminaries he slid his hands over her thighs and lifted her, winding her legs around his body and sinking inside her in a series of hard, determined thrusts.

'Marco…' She cried out his name and he felt the scrape of her fingernails on his shoulders, and then they were moving together, the pleasure so wild and intense that there was no holding back.

He felt her tighten around him, the involuntary spasms of her body driving him forward to his own savage release. As he tumbled over the edge into paradise he gave an agonised groan and thrust hard, his fingers biting into her soft flesh, his mouth locked on hers as he swallowed her cries.

It took him several moments to realise that he was probably hurting her and that water was still thundering down his back. He lowered her carefully and then stroked her soaking hair away from her face.

'Did I hurt you, *amore*?'

'No.' Her voice was a whisper and drops of water clung to her lashes and to her lips. 'You've never hurt me. But I've hurt you, I know I have. I'm sorry for everything, Marco.'

He held her face gently. 'Pain is part of every relationship.'

'I'm sorry,' she whispered again. 'Really sorry that it turned out this way for us.'

'Hush.' He pulled her against him, feeling her tremble, acutely aware of her fragility and vulnerability. 'Everything will be all right, I promise. You will trust me, *tesoro*.'

She stayed like that for a moment, her head against his chest, and then she pulled away. 'We have less than ten minutes before surgery starts.'

He flashed her a smile and reached for a towel. 'Then it is fortunate for both of us that I have an Italian sports car.'

Throughout the whole of Saturday surgery, Amy couldn't stop thinking about Marco. Her body ached from their encounter in the shower and she knew that even though he now understood the real reason for her departure, nothing had changed.

Her last patient of the morning was a mother with a young baby.

'Helen?' Amy smiled and forced herself to concentrate. 'What can I do for you?'

'It's Freddie. I'm so worried about him. He's always been a really sicky baby, but it's getting worse and worse.'

'And how old is he now?' Amy quickly checked the records. 'Six weeks?'

'Yes. He always has brought up milk at the end of his feed.'

'Lots of babies do that.'

'I know but—' Helen broke off and bit her lip. 'I just feel as though something is wrong. He just isn't right, I know he isn't.'

'Let me examine him and see whether I can find anything.' Knowing better than to dismiss a mother's worries, Amy washed her hands and gently lifted the baby out of the car seat. 'I'm sorry to wake you, sweetheart,' she crooned, 'but I want to have a good look at you.'

The baby yawned and stretched then closed his eyes again.

'Is he always this lethargic?' Amy gently undid the poppers on the sleepsuit and undressed the baby down to his nappy.

'Yes. He sleeps all the time.'

Amy examined the baby's abdomen. 'When did you last have him weighed?'

'Last week. He'd lost some weight. The health visitor told

me to increase the feeds, but if I increase the feeds then I just increase the sick. It's got to the point where he's barely keeping anything down.'

Amy slid her hand over the baby's scalp, examining his fontanelle and finding it slightly sunken. 'He seems a bit de-hydrated, Helen. Has he been having plenty of wet nappies?'

'Actually, now you mention it, no.' Helen frowned. 'They used to be quite heavy, but now I sometimes don't even bother changing it because it seems dry. What does that mean?'

'It could mean that he isn't getting enough fluid.'

'Because he's bringing it all up?'

Amy finished the examination, popped him back into his sleepsuit and handed the baby back to Helen. 'You're still breastfeeding?'

'Yes.'

'Wait there just a moment, Helen. I'm going to ask my colleague to have a look at him.'

She tapped on Marco's door and found that he had already finished surgery. 'Can I grab you for a minute?'

'*Sì.*' He leaned back in his chair and gave her a slow, sexy smile. 'Do you want to grab me here or wait until we are home?'

Remembering his performance in the shower, she felt the colour ooze into her cheeks and clearly he read her mind because he raised an eyebrow and his eyes mocked her gently.

'Any time you are ready for a repeat performance, you just have to say the word. Or don't even speak—just switch on the shower and strip naked.'

'Marco!' She glared at him, flustered by the sudden intimacy in his gaze. 'I—I wanted to talk about a patient.'

'I know, but I love to tease you because you always blush. You are the only woman I've ever met who can be hot and shy at the same time.' He leaned back in his chair. 'I am listening, *tesoro*. You need the advice of the master? Superdoctor?'

She looked at him. 'Has a woman ever hit you really, really hard?'

'Such passion.' His smile widened. 'My little English Amy is becoming *al*most Italian.'

'Marco—be serious.'

'I'm serious.' He leaned forward. 'What is your problem, *amore*? Tell me and I will solve it.'

'I have this little baby in my consulting room.'

His smile vanished and he rose to his feet. 'And seeing the baby has upset you? It is too difficult for you emotionally? You want me to handle it?'

Touched by his protectiveness, she shook her head swiftly. 'No, it's nothing like that. It's just that I'm worried about him and I wondered if you'd look at him. He's dehydrated, vomiting after every feed and very, very lethargic. I think he has pyloric stenosis.'

Marco frowned. 'Unlikely. It isn't that common.'

'That's why I wanted you to check him. And you're the one who always taught me to remember the uncommon, particularly when faced by a worried mother.'

'True enough.' He shrugged. 'Have you examined the baby feeding?'

'No.' She shook her head and frowned. 'I didn't think to do that.'

'So—we will do it together.'

They walked back to her consulting room and Marco smiled at Helen. 'You had a good, relaxing Christmas? Plenty of food and wine?'

'I was cooking for twelve so it wasn't exactly relaxing.' Helen gave a wry smile. 'I must admit I'm pretty exhausted. I wondered if that was why Freddie had lost weight. I can't believe my milk is much good at the moment.'

Marco washed his hands. 'You shouldn't have been cooking. Your family should have been pampering you with a little one this age.' He leaned forward and stroked a gentle hand over the baby's head. 'Can I take him?'

Helen nodded and Marco scooped the baby up confidently. 'Are you giving your mother worries?' He gazed down at the baby and gave a faint smile. 'Amazing that something so small can be so much trouble.'

Amy swallowed hard, wishing it wasn't quite so hard watching him with babies.

His gaze shifted from the baby to her and she knew instinctively that he'd followed the direction of her thoughts. He gave her a warm, reassuring smile and her stomach shifted.

What was he thinking?

His eyes searched hers for a moment and then he handed the baby back to Helen. 'Amy is right that the baby is a little dehydrated. You say that he is vomiting after every feed. Is he ready for a feed now?'

'He's a bit sleepy.'

'That might be because he hasn't had enough fluid. Dehydration can make him sleepy. We will undress him a bit—make him a bit less comfortable.' Marco's fingers moved over the baby, undressing, tickling, waking him up, and eventually Freddie yawned. 'So—now try and feed him. He is a man after all, so his stomach is probably a priority for him.'

Helen smiled and put the baby to her breast. Freddie played with the nipple doubtfully and Marco curved a strong hand over the back of the baby's head and guided him gently.

'You are starving hungry, you know you are.'

The baby latched on and Helen looked at Marco. 'He's feeding. Now what?'

'Now I want to look at his tummy.' Marco crouched down and looked at the baby's abdomen. Then he gently felt the stomach. 'Amy? Can you see?' He trailed a finger over the stomach. 'The muscles are straining. They're moving from left to right as they try and push milk through the pylorus. And on the right side I can feel a small, hard lump. You're right, I think. Clever girl.' He rose to his feet and washed his hands.

Helen looked between the two of them. 'So what's wrong with him?'

Amy reached for a piece of paper and a pen. 'We think he has something called pyloric stenosis. Basically it means that the passage between the stomach and the small bowel is narrowed and that stops milk passing into the bowel.' She drew a simple picture to illustrate what she was saying and Helen stared at it.

'But why would that happen?'

'No one really knows. It tends to affect more boys than girls. Has anyone else in your family had the same problem?'

Helen shook her head and Freddie let go of the breast and vomited violently. It cleared Helen's lap and landed on Amy's feet. 'Oh!' Mortified, Helen lifted the baby and reached for a cloth. 'I'm so, so sorry.'

'It's fine, really.' Amy smiled and mopped up the mess with paper towels. 'But I think our diagnosis has just been confirmed.' She looked at Marco. 'Projectile vomiting?'

Helen cuddled Freddie tightly. 'So what happens now?'

'We refer him to the hospital,' Marco said. 'They may want to do more tests—an ultrasound scan, possibly, to get a picture of the muscle.'

'Will that hurt him?'

Marco shook his head. 'It is like the scan they give you in pregnancy.'

'And then what?'

'He will need a small operation to cut through the thickened muscle so that food can then pass into the bowel.'

'An operation?' Helen looked horrified. 'Is it a big one? How long will it take?'

'Probably about half an hour, no more than that. And afterwards he will be given painkillers.'

'I can't bear the thought of him having an operation.' Helen's eyes filled. 'He's so little.'

'But at the moment he can't digest his food,' Amy said gently. 'He needs help, Helen.'

'What a Christmas this has been.' Helen brushed away the tears and sniffed. 'All right. Well, if that's what he needs— when will he have to have it done?'

'Soon, because he is dehydrated.' Marco walked over to Amy's computer. 'We will call the hospital now and talk to the doctors. You should take him straight to the paediatric ward.'

'But it's Saturday!'

'And they will probably put up a drip and give him some fluid.' Marco swiftly completed a referral letter. 'That way they can correct the dehydration before they operate.'

'And when is that likely to be?'

'They will need to check that his blood has the right balance of minerals and salts and then they will operate as soon as possible.'

Helen strapped Freddie back into the car seat and lifted it. 'All right. I'll take him up to the hospital right away. Thank you, both of you.'

'Try not to worry,' Marco said gently, his eyes warm and kind. 'It will all be fine in the end.'

Helen gave a wobbly smile. 'I hope so. Thanks again.'

She left the room, clutching the letter in her hand and Amy sighed. 'Poor thing. What a worry.'

'Yes. Having children also comes with an ocean of worries,' Marco said quietly, walking towards the door. 'Call Paeds. I'll be waiting in the car park for you.'

She sat down at her desk and reached for the phone. 'Why?'

'I need to give you a lift home. We have the rest of the weekend off.'

'And?' *What did he have in mind?*

He smiled. 'First I am going to take you home and wash the vomit off you, then we are going for a bracing walk and finally we are having dinner at the Smugglers' Inn.'

She opened her mouth and closed it again. 'Has anyone ever told you that you're controlling?'

His smile widened. 'I'm a man who knows what he wants, that's true. Don't forget it, *amore*. Now, ring the hospital.'

'I always loved this part of the North Cornish coast.' Amy stared ahead of her, the wind whipping her hair across her face. 'It's wild, isn't it? You can so easily imagine wrecks and smugglers.' She tensed as she felt Marco's arms slide round her.

'It is wild yes, but—' He broke off and gave a shrug that betrayed his Mediterranean heritage. 'Truly? I prefer the beauty of the Amalfi coast. I like to admire the coastline without risking frostbite. One day I will take you to Positano and you will understand what I mean. Positano is a little town that clings to the cliff like a jewel in a necklace. You would love it. And it's very romantic.'

'Positano.' She turned, a smile on her face. 'You sounded so Italian when you said that.'

'*Sì*, because I *am* Italian. So, of course, I sound Italian.' He lowered his mouth to hers and she felt her body melt under the pressure of his kiss. 'Are you ready to go back?'

Still in the circle of his arms, she glanced out to sea again. 'I suppose so.'

'You came here with your grandmother?'

'No. On my own. I used to sit and stare at the waves for hours.'

'That sounds lonely.'

Her whole childhood had been lonely. 'I was used to it.'

'Tell me what made you think you might be infertile.'

Surprised by the sudden change of subject, she looked up at him. 'I had tests.'

'Without telling me?' His eyes darkened ominously and she sighed.

'At the time I didn't think there was anything to tell. To be honest, I didn't really think anything would be wrong.' She wriggled out of his arms, finding it impossible to talk about such a difficult subject when they were so closely entwined. 'We hadn't used any contraception for months—'

'No time at all.'

'I know that.' She took a deep breath. 'But I just had…a bad feeling. It was always a worry of mine.'

'Why would you worry about it? Had you ever tried for a baby before?'

'No.' She threw him a puzzled glance, surprised by the question. 'You know I hadn't.'

'I don't know that. I know very little about your past before you met me.' He reached out, caught a strand of hair that was blowing in front of her face and tucked it behind her ear. 'If I'm honest, I wasn't very interested in your past.'

And she wasn't interested in talking about it.

The touch of his fingers made her stomach tumble and Amy had to force herself to concentrate on the conversation. 'I bumped into a friend of mine who runs an infertility clinic. She suggested I have some tests, so I did.'

'And you didn't think it worth mentioning to me?' Some of the warmth had left his voice and she turned to him.

'You have every right to be angry with me but you have to try and see it from my point of view. If I'd told you, you would have said that it was too soon to worry.'

'It was.'

'No! As it turns out, it wasn't! And I was able to end our marriage quickly.'

'And I'm supposed to be grateful for that?'

'No. Yes.' She wrapped her arms around herself to keep out the cold. 'I don't know. I just know that I ended something that would have ended anyway.'

'You think I would have divorced you for being infertile?' His tone was incredulous. 'Is that truly what you think of me?'

'No, actually.' She turned to him, her voice flat. 'I think you probably would have stayed with me because for all your arrogance and self-confidence you're a decent man and I think you would have felt an obligation. I didn't want that. Only one of us can't have children in this relationship, so there was no need for both of us to suffer.'

His hands closed over her arms and he jerked her against him. 'You think I didn't suffer, *tesoro*?' His eyes blazed into hers. *'You think I didn't suffer when you walked away from me?'*

'I'm sure you did.' The wind howled angrily around them but she ignored it. 'I'm sure you suffered. But nowhere near as much as we both would have suffered if we'd limped along in our marriage.'

He stared down into her face for a moment, as if trying to work something out. Then he released her and his voice was flat. 'It's cold. Let's go home.'

He didn't understand.

And she couldn't expect him to.

Because she hadn't told him who she was or where she'd come from.

Their marriage was doomed, she knew that.

But she'd promised to help out in the practice so she'd work these few weeks and then end it properly. By then she would have been able to convince Marco that it was the right thing for both of them.

They returned from their walk and Marco dragged her into his arms and kissed her, his mouth demanding and passionate. Then he released her suddenly and took a step back-wards. 'Let's go to the Smugglers' Inn.'

'Now?' Still dizzy from his kiss, she looked at him, trying to focus. 'You want to go out?'

'I think it's a good idea. We need to talk. And if we stay here…' he smiled the smile of a red-blooded male '…we won't talk. Even I won't be tempted to make love to you in front of the locals so we'll talk on neutral territory.'

'There's really nothing left to say, Marco. We don't have to go out. I could cook something.'

'Out of what?' He gave a humourless laugh. 'Have you checked in the fridge, Amy? Housekeeping isn't exactly my strong point at the best of times and these certainly aren't the best of times. Unless you nipped out between patients, I'm guessing that you haven't been to the supermarket either?'

His accent was more than usually pronounced and she gave a soft smile. 'No, I haven't. And you don't have to tell me that housekeeping isn't your strong point. You've always been a very traditional Italian male. You want your woman in the kitchen.'

And she'd loved that.

She'd loved the fact that she had finally been able to create a home.

She glanced around her, at the house she'd chosen, *the place she'd wanted to raise their children.*

His eyes trapped hers and he inhaled deeply. 'Not *that* traditional,' he said huskily. 'I was more than happy for you to pursue a career if that was truly what you wanted. But it wasn't, was it?'

She shifted. 'Do you want to argue about this now or shall we go to the pub?'

'Subject avoidance appears to be your favourite activity at the moment.' He gave a shake of his head. 'Let's go to the pub. Give me five minutes to change.'

Deciding that jeans were perfectly acceptable for a casual supper at the Smugglers' Inn, Amy didn't bother changing but went into her bathroom, splashed her face with cold water and applied some make-up. Remembering everyone's comments on how pale she was, she gave her cheeks an extra swipe with the blusher brush and then decided that she looked like a clown and rubbed it off again.

She was pale, yes. But apart from that she looked quite normal. Nothing like a woman whose insides were in turmoil and whose heart was breaking.

'Ready?' Marco stood in the doorway, a black jumper brushing the hard lines of his jaw, his eyes glittering dangerously. There was fire and confrontation in his eyes and Amy swallowed, remembering the passion that had exploded between them that morning. *And the previous evening.*

Perhaps they were right to go out.

They couldn't just carry on making love, could they? What did that solve? Nothing. If anything, it made things worse. They were becoming more and more entwined in the emotional web they were spinning and before long it would be almost impossible to extricate themselves.

Realising that the evening wasn't going to be easy, Amy gave a sigh as she followed him out of the room and waited while he locked the front door.

It was dark and cold and she snuggled deeper into her coat.

'Do you think it's going to snow again?' She slid into the Maserati, enjoying the warmth and the smell of leather.

'I have no idea.' Marco waited while she closed the door. 'I hope not. The car hates it. I hate it. The only place I want snow is when I'm skiing and there isn't much of that on the North Cornish coast.'

Amy smiled at the thought of skiing in Penhally. 'The car is still working, then, despite the cold?'

'*Sì*, occasionally.' Humour in his voice, Marco leaned across and fastened her seat belt then slid his hands over the steering-wheel in a gesture of affection. 'Except when she wants to make my life difficult. Which, of course, she does quite often.' The engine gave a throat roar and Marco steered the car onto the coast road.

'Why is it a "she"? Why does it have to be a woman?'

'Of course she is a woman.' Smoothly he changed gear, his eyes fixed on the road. 'You only have to look at her tempera-ment. She's moody sometimes. Unpredictable. Determined to frustrate. And then other times—she is a dream.' He spoke with such affection that she looked at him with disbelief.

'Marco Avanti, you're a qualified doctor, not a little boy with a toy. You're just a little bit crazy, do you know that?'

He turned his head quickly and gave her a sexy smile. 'Crazy is good, no? Sensible is…' He removed one hand from the wheel and slid it over her knee. 'English? No passion. No emotion.'

Feeling the sudden rush of heat inside her body, Amy coloured, relieved that it was dark. Everything she knew about passion and emotion she'd learned from him. Her response to him had always astonished her. It was as if he drew out a part of her that she hadn't known existed.

'We're so different. How did we ever end up together?'

'Because what we have is powerful.' He increased speed and she gripped the edge of the seat and gasped.

'Marco! Are you planning to end the year with a speed-ing ticket?'

'Calm down. This car spends so long in the garage that she needs a run occasionally. And, anyway, the police have better things to do than check my speed.' Marco swooped into the car park and turned off the engine.

Feeling relieved that they were still alive, Amy undid her seat belt. *If he were less macho, would it be easier to resist him?*

Or was it his blatant, unashamed masculinity that was so attractive?

Marco was red-blooded male, through and through. Women sensed it within moments of meeting him. *She'd* sensed it.

She shivered as she slammed the car door and felt the wind whip round her body. 'It's cold.' She felt his arm slide round her and then he was urging her across the car park and into the welcoming warmth of the pub.

'*Buenas noches*, Marco,' Tony called out from the bar, and Marco sighed.

'You just wished me goodnight in Spanish, my friend. *Buona sera* is Italian. Don't you ever listen to anything I tell you?'

'Depends what it is.' Tony reached for a glass, a smile on his face. 'If you're telling me to eat less fat, no, I don't listen. If you're ordering a drink, my hearing improves.'

Marco glanced around the pub. 'It's quiet.'

'Early yet. Most folks are still tucked up indoors, away from the weather. It'll be crowded later. Always is. What will it be? Amy?'

'I'll have fizzy water.'

Tony lifted an eyebrow at Marco. 'Is she going to be decent company on fizzy water?'

Marco gave a slow, masculine smile. 'Unlike most of you Englishmen, I don't need to get my women drunk in order to seduce them. My company alone is enough.'

His comment was so outrageously arrogant that Amy couldn't hold back her laughter and he turned towards her, his attention caught, his expression curious. 'What is funny?'

'*You're* funny. You make me laugh. You always did.' Realising that paying him compliments wasn't going to help create distance between them, she turned away quickly and settled herself at the table by the fire. 'Nice fire, Tony.'

'Are you two eating? Specials are up on the board.'

Amy stared at the scrawl on the blackboard, wondering if she dared admit she wasn't hungry. There was something about being in love with Marco that just drove her appetite away.

'I'll have the goat's cheese salad,' she muttered, and Marco frowned.

'She'll have lamb hotpot. And I will, too.' He sat down opposite her and Amy gaped at him.

'I don't want lamb hotpot!'

'Amy.' His voice was patient. 'You look as though you've eaten nothing for the past two years. This morning you missed breakfast. The sandwich that Kate gave you at lunchtime came back uneaten. You are eating less than that baby we referred to the hospital. Tonight you're having lamb hotpot and you're eating it, even if I have to fork it into your mouth myself.'

'But I'm not—'

'Not hungry?' He finished the sentence for her and gave a nod of understanding. 'So—something is the matter? You are off your food because you are so in love with me you can't see straight, no?'

'Don't start, Marco. I don't love you. And you don't love me. Not enough.'

He studied her face in silence. 'All right. Because I need you to recover your appetite, we'll play a different game for the time being.' He leaned back, his dark eyes glittering in the light of the fire. 'I tell you one thing you don't know about me and you tell me one thing I don't know about you.'

'I don't like lamb hotpot. There.' She smiled innocently. 'That's my one thing. Now it's your turn.'

'I don't like really skinny women?'

She laughed. 'You should do an article for the local paper. It would help soothe all those poor women sobbing over the extra pounds they gained over Christmas.'

'Only women think that thin is attractive. All men prefer curves.'

Tony delivered the hotpot to the table and Amy sighed as she picked up her fork and looked at it without enthusiasm. 'Why is it that you always get your own way, Marco?'

'Because I'm always right?' His expression grew serious. 'I didn't get my own way when you left, Amy. That wasn't what I wanted.'

She stilled, the fork balanced in her fingers, her heart in her throat. 'I thought we weren't going to talk about this now.'

'You made the decision for both of us, just as I did with the hotpot.' His eyes challenged her. 'You didn't like it when I chose your food.'

'That's not the same thing at all.'

'You're right, it isn't. To select someone's meal for them...' he waved a hand dismissively '...that is nothing, I agree. But to choose someone's whole future—now, that's entirely different, *amore*.'

'That's not fair, Marco. A relationship can't work if one of the people involved doesn't want it to work. And I didn't— it wasn't what I wanted.'

'You're lying. You wanted it but you were afraid.' He leaned forward. 'My beautiful, cowardly Amy. You were afraid that infertility would wreck our marriage. So you wrecked it anyway. That is woman logic.'

'Woman logic?'

'*Sì.*' He dug into the hot pot. 'A man would not wreck something just in case.'

She inhaled deeply. 'It wasn't "just in case."'

'Eat.'

'But—'

'Eat, Amy, or I will have to force-feed you.'

She sighed and stabbed a small amount of food with her fork.

Marco sighed. 'Now put it in your mouth—yes, like that. Good. And now another mouthful. These tests you had done—I want to know what they told you.'

Amy stopped chewing and put down her fork. 'I had the usual done. The laparoscopy—'

'You had a laparoscopy?' He interrupted her, his tone rough. 'When? How? Where was I?'

'Busy. Working.' She shrugged. 'I don't know.'

The breath hissed through his teeth. 'All right—carry on. You had a laparoscopy. And then?'

'I had mild endometriosis. Nothing that needed treating. Just enough to have completely blocked my Fallopian tubes.' Her hand shaking, Amy picked up her fork again.

'So the laparoscopy suggested that your Fallopian tubes were not patent, is that right?'

'That's right.'

'Eat.'

Amy stared at the food on her fork. 'I really don't think I—'

'Eat.'

Aware that the pub was filling up and that a few people were glancing towards them, Amy dutifully took another mouthful of food. 'I'm not hungry.'

'Then you need to do more vigorous exercise, *amore*, increase that appetite of yours,' Marco purred softly, and her eyes flew to his.

'No, we mustn't. We mustn't do that again,' she whispered softly, and he lifted an eyebrow.

'And why not?'

'Because it is just confusing things.'

'I'm not confused.' He gave a slow, sexy smile and reached across the table and took her fork from her hand. 'I know exactly what I want. And I know exactly what you want, too, *tesoro.*'

'I want a divorce.' She heard his sigh and bit her lip. 'Marco, I know that we have fun together and I know that the sex is good.' She glanced swiftly towards the crowd at the bar but no one was paying them any attention. 'But our relationship can't carry on. It's over.'

The humour was gone from his eyes. 'It isn't over. We met and the chemistry was so powerful that for three days we didn't get out of bed. We made love almost continuously. Do you remember that, *amore*?'

Of course she remembered that. 'Perhaps that was the problem. We let the sex cloud our judgement. Sharing a bed is very different from sharing a life.'

'So you're still pretending that there is no emotional connection between us and never was?'

Trying to ignore the faint sarcasm in his tone, she straightened her back and didn't look at him. 'I like you, of course—'

'Amy, a woman doesn't lose her appetite over a serious case of "like". You were in love with me and you are still in love with me. Please, at least admit that.'

Her stomach churned. 'Answer me one question, Marco.' She pushed her plate away from her. 'How many times has a woman ended a relationship with you?'

'Never.'

Finally she looked at him. 'That's what I thought. So perhaps it's just very difficult for you to accept that I want to end the relationship.'

'You're implying that this is all about my ego?' He let out a long breath and shook his head in blatant disbelief. 'Sometimes, Amy, you are more trouble than the Maserati and that, as you say in English, is really saying something. Now, eat and forget our problems.'

Reluctantly Amy took a few more forkfuls of food. 'It's quite good,' she conceded, 'for hotpot.'

'*Sì*. And you are going to eat all of it. You're a good cook. Who taught you? Your mother?'

'No, my grandmother. She loved cooking, especially baking. Her cakes were amazing. She was quite a homely, domestic person. My mother wasn't.' Discovering that she was hungrier than she'd thought, Amy slowly ate her way through the bowl of food.

'Why did you stay with her on your own? Did your mother never join you?'

'She was always working and she needed somewhere for me to go during the holidays. And, anyway, they didn't get on. They had a difference of opinion.'

'About what?'

'About me. My mother never really wanted children.' Talking about herself felt uncomfortable and with a flash of panic she swiftly she changed the subject. 'How's Michelle Watson? Is she home from hospital?'

'Yes, and they have changed her asthma medication.' He gave a twisted smile. 'Poor Carol worries so much about her. I'm planning to call and see her tomorrow.'

'It's Sunday.'

'Sunday is the only day I have time to fit in that sort of visit. I need to check on her. She needs the support. And I also want to check on Lizzie.'

'They certainly didn't seem like a perfectly harmonious family.' Amy glanced around to check that no one was listening to them and then lowered her voice. 'I wondered whether Lizzie might be suffering from more than teenage tantrums.'

'Me, too. But it wasn't right to tackle the subject when the focus was on her sister.'

'Half-sister.'

'You think that might be the root of the problem?'

'I don't know. I suppose I'd start there.'

He nodded agreement. 'I will find a way of spending time with her tomorrow.'

Amy felt a warm rush of pride. 'You're a good doctor, Marco Avanti,' she said softly. 'You care about the children so much, I know.'

'And with that comment you have brought us back to our own problems. You are imagining that my life would be empty without my own children and that I'd therefore be better with a different woman.' He finished his food and put down his fork. 'Despite the fact you are an intelligent woman, you are putting two and two together and coming up with the wrong answer.'

She knew it wasn't the wrong answer.

She knew that from personal experience just how child-lessness could affect a marriage, but she wasn't ready to share that with him.

She'd never shared it with anyone. 'Do you miss paediatrics?'

'Sometimes. But I see a great number of the children in the practice and it is nice to have that long-term relationship so...' he shrugged '...in many ways I am very happy as a family doctor.'

'You've done a good job with the practice, you and Nick. It must have been awful after Annabel died.' She bit her lip. 'I—I didn't know or I would have written sooner.'

'He managed. I managed.' Marco shrugged again. 'The surgery carried on.'

'Kate's such a good practice manager.'

'Yes.' Marco finished his drink. 'Although I'm not sure how long she'll stay.'

'Really? She's thinking of leaving? Why?'

'I don't know that she's thinking of leaving. It is just a suspicion and I might be wrong. I just sense that things aren't altogether good for her at the moment.'

'Well, being a single mother must be hard,' Amy said quietly, and Marco nodded, his eyes on hers.

'And losing someone you love is even harder. All the more reason not to throw it away when you find it. Let's go home, *amore*. It is more comfortable to argue at home.'

But they didn't argue.

They made love and then talked long into the night. And Marco didn't mention loving or leaving. He just seduced and possessed her until she was no longer capable of rational thought.

Until she'd forgotten why it was that she had to leave.

CHAPTER NINE

ON MONDAY Amy worked her way through a steady flow of patients, but couldn't stop thinking about the visit she and Marco had made to see little Michelle the day before. There had been no sign of Lizzie and Carol had told them in an embarrassed voice that the teenager had come in drunk the night before and was sleeping it off. So Marco had merely checked on Michelle and reassured Carol, but Amy knew that he was still determined to spend some time with Lizzie.

'Amy?' The door opened and Nick walked into her consulting room. 'I've been thinking about the conversation we had on Friday afternoon. I think you need to tell Marco the truth.'

Still wondering about Lizzie, Amy pulled her mind back to the present. 'I've told him.'

'Ah.' He looked at her expectantly. 'And?'

'And nothing. It doesn't change anything just because he knows. Our marriage is still over.' She almost laughed as she listened to herself and recalled the passion of the weekend. For a marriage that was over, the relationship was intensely passionate.

And she was making trouble for herself, she knew she was. The web was tightening.

Nick looked startled. 'That's what Marco wants?'

'Well, no, not exactly.' Amy fiddled with her pen, 'He doesn't think he wants it, but I know it's the best thing for both of us.'

'You're deciding for both of you again? On what basis?'

On the basis of her past. On the basis that she had first-hand experience in this area.

Dark memories oozed into her brain and she pushed them away resolutely. 'Yes,' she croaked, 'I am deciding for both of us. Once Kate finds a locum, I'll be off.'

'Does Marco know you still feel like this?'

'I keep telling him. He doesn't seem to be listening.'

Nick grimaced. 'That sounds like Marco. He has a way of ploughing through obstacles that get in the way of what he wants. He did it when we were setting up this place. You might find he changes your mind yet.'

'That isn't going to happen.' *She couldn't let it happen.* 'In the meantime, I'll do the job you're paying me to do.'

Nick stood for a moment. 'This must be very hard for you, Amy. If you need a shoulder…' He gave a wry smile and raked a hand through his hair. 'I'm not sure that relationship counselling is my forte, but—'

'I'm fine, Nick,' she said quietly, 'but thank you. I'll manage on my own.'

The way she'd always managed. It was what she did. The way she lived her life.

The whole of Penhally came to life on New Year's Eve.

Despite another small flurry of snow and the drop in temperature, the shops were crowded as people rushed around, preparing for the celebrations. The off licence did a steady trade as people bought bottles of champagne and then picked their way home along the snowy pavements, bottles clanking in plastic bags, their breath clouding the freezing air.

The surgery was also busy and it was almost the end of the

day before Amy managed to find time to nip to the staffroom
for a cup of tea.

'You, too?' Kate followed her into the staffroom and filled
the kettle. 'If I don't have a cup of tea this minute, my throat
is going to collapse in protest. The pavements are icy and
we've had several people in after falls, but at least the wind
has dropped, which is good news. The firework display
should be able to go ahead. They've brought it forward to six
o'clock so that the children can enjoy it. Everyone will have
time to go home and get changed before the party at the
Penhally Arms. What are you wearing?'

Amy hesitated. 'I'm not going.'

Kate gaped at her. 'Not going? Amy, you *have* to go. It's
the event of the year. Well, maybe not quite the year, but it's
certainly the event of the winter.' She gave a rueful smile. 'Not
that that's saying much around here. We're a bit short of
entertainment on the long, dark nights, as you well know.'

'I can't go, Kate.' Amy took two mugs from the cupboard
and Kate dropped a tea bag in each. 'It would just be too
awkward.'

'Why? What's awkward about it?' Kate poured water into
the mugs. 'You're working here, aren't you? You're living
with Marco. Everyone knows you're together—'

'We're not together. Not in the way you mean.'

'Oh. I hoped…' Kate finished making the tea and took it
with her to the nearest chair. 'Well, anyway, it's just a party,
Amy. I don't understand the problem. Do you have a dress?'

'No.' Amy thought about the contents of the wardrobe. *The
wardrobe she'd abandoned along with that whole part of her
life.* 'Well, yes, I suppose I do have a dress, but it isn't really
suitable. I mean, it isn't me any more.'

Kate sipped her tea. 'Was it you once upon a time?'

Without thinking she answered. 'Oh, yes. It was Marco's
favourite. Whenever I wore it we never actually managed

to—' She broke off, suddenly embarrassed by how much she'd revealed, but Kate simply chuckled.

'You never actually managed to leave the house in it? If it was that good, you should definitely wear it to the party tonight. In fact, I insist on it. If you don't turn up wearing it I'm going to drive you home myself and force you to change.'

Amy sighed and shook her head. 'I don't think the dress sends out the right message.'

'What does that matter?' Kate's tone was dry. 'Since when did men take any notice of the messages we give them, anyway? Especially men like Marco. Whatever the dress is saying, Marco will hear what he wants to hear, take it from me. He's that kind of guy.'

Amy's stomach lurched alarmingly and she wondered fleetingly just how well Kate knew Marco. *Kate was an attractive woman.*

And then she pushed the thought away. Kate and Marco had been colleagues for two years. It was natural that they'd know each other quite well.

And she had no right to be possessive. She was letting him go. 'I honestly don't think a party is the right way to spend an evening.'

'Are things that bad?' Kate's voice was gentle. 'I was really hoping that the two of you might have patched up your marriage.'

'We haven't.'

'I'm sorry. And surprised. You're so good together and you've been laughing and you make a great team. I thought you were getting on well.'

'We *are* getting on well.' Amy thought of their passionate love-making and blushed. 'But we haven't patched up our marriage.'

Kate studied her. 'Why not? You're so in love with him, anyone can see that. And he's in love with you!'

Amy frowned. 'Nick said the same thing—'

Kate tensed slightly, her eyes suddenly wary. 'Did he?' Her tone was suddenly cool. 'You've discussed this with Nick?'

'He's surprisingly intuitive, don't you think?'

'Sometimes. With patients.' Kate stood up so suddenly that her coffee sloshed over the table. 'Oh, now look what I've done.' She walked across to the sink and picked up a cloth and Amy watched, mystified by the sudden tension in the air. Everything had been fine until she'd mentioned the senior partner's name.

'Has something happened between you and Nick?' *Had they had a row?* Or was it something more than that?

'Nothing. You know what this place is like. We're in each other's pockets all the time.' She wiped the table. 'So, if Marco *was* in love with you, would you stay?'

'No. I'd be leaving even if he was in love with me.' Amy paused. 'I can't have children. That's why I left and it's why I'll be leaving again. I can't give Marco the family he needs.' Swiftly, removing as much of the emotion as possible, she told Kate the facts and the older woman sank back onto the chair, her expression sympathetic.

'Oh, Amy, I'm so sorry. Why didn't you tell me any of this before? You must have gone through so much and all on your own!'

'I couldn't talk to anyone about it,' Amy murmured. 'I— I'm not really used to talking about problems and this, well, this was just too big.'

'But there are so many options these days and even if none of them worked, there's always adoption.'

Amy tightened her grip on her mug.

Why did people always say that?

Why did they throw it in like some sort of consolation prize with no emotional value?

'That wouldn't be a solution. It's hard to understand, I

know.' She rose to her feet quickly. 'I'd better get back. Surgery was very busy. I have some notes to tie up and some referral letters to write.'

'If I've upset you, I'm sorry.' Kate's voice was soft. 'I probably understand more than you think, Amy. Not about the infertility, no. I don't pretend to know what that must be like. But I know all about finding the man you truly love and then not being able to be with him. Life has a warped sense of humour. Whoever said that it was better to have loved and lost than never to have loved at all, had obviously never loved. Either that or he was on drugs when he wrote that. Love is agony.'

Amy stood for a moment, unsure what to say. Was Kate referring to the tragic loss of her husband years earlier? Or something else entirely?

She opened her mouth to ask a probing question but then the door opened and Alison walked in.

'Is that kettle hot? My tongue is sticking to the roof of my mouth.'

Amy looked at Kate for a moment longer and the practice manager gave a tired smile.

'Go and finish your paperwork, Amy, or I'll be forced to nag you.'

In other words, this wasn't the right time for a deep conversation. Knowing that Kate was right, Amy smiled at Alison.

'Kettle is hot.'

'Aren't you getting ready to go out? The party started half an hour ago.' Marco paused in the doorway, looking at Amy who was curled up on the sofa with a book that she wasn't reading.

She couldn't concentrate on anything. When she wasn't working, all she did was think about Marco. 'You go.'

'We're both going.' He reached out a hand and pulled her to her feet.

'I'm tired, Marco.'

He gave a slow smile and stroked a hand over her cheek. 'Too much sex perhaps. Tonight, *tesoro*, I will let you sleep. I promise.'

She blushed. 'Marco, I just don't want to go to the Penhally Arms! Everyone will be there.'

'*Sì.*' He pulled her towards the stairs. 'That is why we are going. We're part of this community.'

'You are. I'm not.'

He jerked her against him. 'You're my wife,' he breathed, his eyes holding hers. 'Remember that.'

'Marco—' She broke off and sighed. This wasn't the time to start that argument again. 'All right, I'll come to the party if it means so much to you.'

'Good.' He lowered his head and delivered a lingering kiss to her mouth. 'We leave in ten minutes.'

Amy waited for him to walk into the shower and then opened the wardrobe and took out the dress. It was scarlet, daring, and didn't match her mood at all.

If she were dressing for her mood then it would have been black, she thought gloomily, looking in the wardrobe to see what else there was.

But there was nothing.

Only the vivid red dress.

With a little shrug she slipped it on, wondering if it would even still fit.

'*Molto belissima,*' Marco breathed from behind her, sliding his hands slowly over her hips and then drawing her zip upwards in a smooth movement. 'I always *loved* you in this dress.'

'It isn't— I don't—'

'It is and you should.' He turned her to face him. 'Tonight

let's just go out and have a good time. Forget everything. No mention of problems. Agreed?'

She hesitated and then nodded. It sounded good to her. She was exhausted. 'All right.'

The Penhally Arms was decorated with clusters of balloons and rows of twinkling lights and the dining room had been cleared to accommodate a dance floor. Although it was still relatively early, the place was already crowded.

'So now you will see all my moves and be unable to resist me.' Smiling wickedly, Marco hauled her straight onto the dance floor and spun her round.

'What are you doing?' Half laughing, half embarrassed, she moved closer to him and he shrugged.

'Dancing. Your dress has a very sexy split at the side. When I spin you round I get a better view of your legs.'

'Marco, that's dreadful!'

'Not from where I'm standing.' He pulled her against him and ran a possessive hand over the curve of her bottom, leaving everyone in no doubt that their marriage was alive and well.

'People are watching everything you do.'

'Let them watch. The only way to survive in a small community is not to fight it. Don't be so English.' He smiled down at her, his eyes glittering dark and dangerous in the dim light. 'Relax and let go. All the people here wish us well.'

And, indeed, everyone seemed happy and contented, mingling, drinking and eating. Amy joined Marco as he weaved his way through them, exchanging a few words of greeting here and there, stopping to have a longer conversation with some people.

And then she saw Kate standing in the doorway, a look of such utter yearning on her face that Amy stopped dead. Puzzled, she followed the direction of Kate's gaze and gave a soft gasp of enlightenment.

Marco turned from his argument about Italian wines. 'What?'

'I just— I didn't...' She drew him to one side, her voice soft. 'Kate. Did you see the way she looked at Nick?'

'No, but I can imagine.'

Amy looked up at him. 'I think she's in love with him.'

'I *know* she's in love with him.'

'You *know*?'

'I have worked with both of them for over two years,' Marco said wearily. 'I may be a man, but even I can pick up on tension and atmosphere if it surrounds me for long enough.'

'Well, but— That's great.' Amy smiled, genuinely delighted for Kate. 'I mean, they're both widowed and—'

Marco pressed a finger over her lips. 'I think the situation is perhaps more complicated than it might first appear to be,' he drawled softly, removing his finger and giving her a gentle kiss instead. 'Say nothing to either of them.'

'But Kate is my friend—'

'All right, then say nothing to Nick,' Marco said quietly, his gaze resting on his colleague who was standing at the bar, talking to several other locals. 'Nick is a man with a lot of issues.'

'You mean he still hasn't got over Annabel's death?'

Marco was silent for a moment. 'That, yes. And more, I suspect. Come on, let's eat.'

They helped themselves to food, chatted to some of the villagers and then everyone started the countdown to midnight.

'Ten, nine eight...' everyone chanted in unison, and then the church bells started to chime and they all let out an enormous cheer.

Amy smiled and suddenly she was glad she'd come. Just because you knew that tomorrow was going to be difficult, it didn't mean that you couldn't grab hold of today and enjoy it.

'*Felice Anno Nuovo.*' Marco took her in his arms and kissed her. 'Happy New Year, *amore.*'

Amy closed her eyes, her happiness bitter-sweet. '*Felice Anno Nuovo*, Marco.'

She didn't have any reason to believe that the new year would be any happier than the last two, but Marco had insisted that tonight wasn't about their relationship and she had to admit that it had been nice to get away from the subject for a while.

All around her people were hugging and kissing and letting off party poppers, and then she saw Kate and Nick. And there was something about the way they stood—*so close but neither touching nor talking*—that made Amy catch her breath.

Across the lively crowd, she could almost feel their agony. *Couldn't anyone else feel it, too?*

She glanced around her to see if anyone else had noticed but everyone was dancing and singing and whooping.

And suddenly, Nick finished his drink, picked up his coat and strode out of the bar, his handsome face strained and his mouth grim. He had his car keys in his hand and one glance at the misery in Kate's eyes told Amy that he was going home alone.

Moments later Kate picked up her bag and followed, clearly too distressed to stay at the party.

Amy watched the door of the pub close behind her and hesitated.

Should she follow? Or should she stay out of it?

She'd seen the tears in Kate's eyes and knew that she was close to breaking down. Who did she have to turn to?

Around her everyone was celebrating noisily and Marco was in conversation with a group of people, so Amy quietly slipped away, intending to offer Kate some support.

Outside, the winter wind bit through her thin dress and suddenly she wished she'd stopped to pick up her coat.

Then she saw Kate, hurrying across the car park towards Nick. 'Nick! Wait.' Her voice carried and Amy watched as Nick paused, his hand on the door of his car, the collar of his coat turned up against the bitter chill of the wind.

Laughter burst from inside the pub but the two of them didn't even look round.

Were they talking?

What were they saying?

Amy knew she should go back into the pub but she just couldn't look away and she gave a soft intake of breath as she saw Nick's hand lift towards Kate's shoulder as if he was going to pull her against him. For a moment his hand hovered, and then his fingers curled into a fist and his hand dropped to his side.

Without saying another word to Kate, he slid into his car and slammed the door.

Nick drove off with an ominous squeal of tyres and Kate stood for a long, tortured moment, her back to Amy.

And then finally she turned and Amy saw tears glistening on her face.

'Why did you go outside?' Marco slid his coat over Amy and turned up the heater in the car. 'Were you hoping for hypothermia?'

'I was worried about Kate.' Her teeth chattering, Amy snuggled under his coat. 'She looked…desperate. Do you think we should call on her?'

'We can't solve everyone's problems, Amy.' He drove carefully on the icy roads. 'We don't even seem to be managing to solve our own.'

'There's nothing to solve.'

'We have a major difference of opinion. You love me, Amy. Admit that at least.'

Exhausted with lying, Amy looked at him. 'All right, I love

you. There, I said it. Are you satisfied?' She turned her head away from him. 'I said it and it still doesn't change a thing. We can't be together.'

'Because you think you can't have children? We're not the first couple to face this and it doesn't have to be the death of our relationship.'

The conversation continued all the way home and followed them into the house.

'If the whole children thing bothers you that much, let's talk about it.' Marco dropped his keys on the table and strode through to the kitchen. 'There are any number of options. IVF. Adoption.'

'That isn't an option.'

'Why not?'

She hesitated. 'Because it still wouldn't be your child.'

'I want you, Amy. You. I take you as you are.' Marco jammed his fingers into his hair and let out a stream of Italian that was completely incomprehensible, but the gist of it was clear even to her. He was frustrated and exasperated. '*What* do I have to do to convince you?'

'Nothing. You'll never convince me. That's why I left, Marco.' Her voice was soft. 'There was really nothing left to say.'

CHAPTER TEN

THE first two weeks of the new year were flat and bleak. Children scurried along the pavements wearing hats and scarves on their way back to school, everyone removed the Christmas decorations and all that was left of the festive period was icy cold weather and frosty streets.

In the Penhally Bay Surgery, the atmosphere was tense. Amy woke up feeling exhausted every day and was beginning to wonder whether she'd contracted a virus in Africa. Marco refused to listen to her reminders that she was leaving in just two more weeks. Nick seemed more aloof than ever and although Kate was her usual efficient self, her face was pale and she hardly ever seemed to smile.

Unable to forget the scene she'd witnessed on New Year's Eve, Amy tried to talk to her, but they were so busy that it wasn't until the third week of January that Amy finally caught her on her own as they were leaving work.

'Do you fancy a coffee?'

'Now?' Kate glanced at her watch. 'I suppose I could. My babysitter doesn't leave for another hour. All right. Why not?'

They went to the nearest coffee-shop and found a small table in the window. 'You're sure you're leaving at the end of the month?' Kate unwound her scarf and picked at the foam on her cappuccino. 'I had a call from Adam Donnelly today, confirming his arrival date.'

Amy felt her stomach drop. It was one thing to know that she was leaving, quite another to actually do it. 'Yes. I have no choice.'

'For what it's worth, I think you're wrong. What you have with Marco is strong enough to withstand everything.'

Amy shook her head. 'I don't want to talk about me. I want to talk about you. Kate…' she leaned forward, her eyes gentle '…how long have you been in love with Nick?'

Pain flickered in Kate's eyes. 'Is it worth me uttering a denial?'

'No. Because I saw the two of you together on New Year's Eve.'

'Ah…' Kate gave a twisted smile. 'That was a particularly bad evening. Nick at his least communicative. Believe me, that's saying something.'

'He doesn't communicate? But you're always talking. You and he.' Amy frowned, confused. 'You're *always* planning and laughing.'

'That's business. Never personal.'

'But you'd like it to be personal.'

Kate stared down at her coffee. 'It's complicated, Amy. I can't tell you all of it. But…' She hesitated. 'I will tell you that I've decided to leave. I can't do this any more. I just can't work alongside him, it hurts too much. There. You're the only person I've said that to. I'd be grateful if you didn't repeat it until I've decided for sure what I want to do.'

'You want to leave? No! You can't do that!' Amy reached across the table and took her hand. 'You love your job. You love working with Nick. You're a great team.'

Kate pulled her hand away. 'There's only so much torture a woman can stand, Amy. I've reached my limit.'

'Are you quite sure he doesn't feel the same way about you?'

Kate stared blindly into her coffee. 'Does Nick feel anything for me? Yes, I think he probably does. Is he going to do anything about it? No, definitely not. He isn't that sort of man.'

'Has he dated anyone since Annabel died?'

'Oh, yes.' Kate gave a bitter laugh. 'Quite a few women, actually. Just no one who is remotely interested in creating an emotional connection. That isn't Nick.'

'Does he know you're thinking of leaving?'

'No.' Kate picked up her coffee. 'I'm going to tell him soon, though. I need to do something different. Goodness knows what. Get a life, as my son would say. Stop brooding. Nick's only a man after all.'

'But some men are harder to get out of your system than others.'

Kate looked at her and gave a sad smile. 'Yes. And you'd understand that, wouldn't you, Amy?'

'Kate tells me that Adam Donnelly is starting in a week.' Wondering why she was always so exhausted, Amy slid her bag onto her shoulder. 'Finally you'll have a proper replacement for Lucy.'

'You're still intent on leaving, then? Despite everything?' Marco's glance burned a hole in her conscience and she forced herself to carry on walking towards the car.

'Yes. Of course. I've told you that all along.'

His phone buzzed and Marco gave a tired sigh and answered it. 'Marco Avanti.' He listened for a moment and then his jaw tightened. 'We'll come over now.'

'What?' Amy looked at him as he dropped the phone back into his pocket and strode towards his car.

'That was Carol. Lizzie is screaming with a headache and she has spots. She's worried that she has meningitis.'

'Meningitis?'

Marco shrugged and unlocked the car. 'We will see. Are you coming?'

'Of course! Why wouldn't I?'

'Because you're leaving, Amy, remember? In another week the inhabitants of Penhally will no longer be your responsibility.'

They sat in silence, Marco's hands gripping the steering-wheel tightly as he drove the short distance to the terraced cottage that Carol shared with her husband and the two girls.

'Thank you so much for coming.' Carol's voice was thick with tears as she let them into the house. 'I always seem to be ringing you. My phone is programmed to ring your number.'

'How long has she had the headache?'

'Well, she was out with her friends last night and they were obviously drinking. Again.' Carol's mouth tightened. 'She's grounded, but that's another story. Last night when she came in she was really drunk—slurring her words and really, really stroppy. Worse than ever. I left her to sleep it off and, of course, she woke up with a headache. Nothing surprising there. I assumed it was a hangover but it's just got worse and worse and about an hour ago she started complaining that the light hurt her eyes. That's when I noticed this rash on her face and I panicked.'

'She is in the bedroom?' Marco was already on the stairs and Amy was right behind him.

'She can't get out of bed because her head is so bad. Her bedroom is the second door on the right.'

The teenager was lying on her side, crying softly, and little Michelle was curled up on the bed next to her sister.

''Izzie sick,' she muttered, and Carol hastily scooped the child off the bed.

'You shouldn't be there. You might catch something. Go downstairs to Daddy, sweetheart. Pete? Can you come and take the baby?'

Reluctant to be parted from her sister, Michelle reached out her arms. ''Izzie sick.'

Marco slid a hand over her cheek. ''Izzie is going to be fine, *cucciola mia*. Go with your mama.'

'I'll be right back,' Carol said, but Marco shook his head.

'I'd like to examine Lizzie and talk to her on my own first. Amy will help me.'

Carol hesitated and then gave a nod. 'All right. I'll be downstairs with Michelle if you need me.'

'Where she always is,' Lizzie sniffed, her forearm across her eyes as she rolled onto her back. 'If you ever want to find Mum, just look for Michelle.' Her face was red and blotchy from crying and Amy noticed the spots on her face. 'My head is killing me. It's like a bomb is exploding in it every minute. Am I dying?'

Marco sat down on the edge of the bed. 'You're not dying,' he said gently, 'but I'll take a look at you and then we'll talk.'

'Oh, don't you start,' Lizzie groaned, rolling onto her side again. 'When adults say "talk" they mean "nag". Don't drink, don't stay out late, don't spend time with those friends because they're not suitable—who the hell does she think she is, anyway, picking my friends? Life is just a load of bloody "don'ts".'

'Is that how it seems?'

'It's how it is.' Lizzie screwed up her face and started to cry. 'God, my head hurts. Mum said I might have meningitis. That's why she got Michelle out of here. She doesn't care about me, but she doesn't want her baby hurt.' The teenager put her hands over her face but Amy saw tears find their way through her fingers.

'You're her baby, too.' Marco opened his bag and took out a stethoscope and an ophthalmoscope.

'No, I'm just a reminder of Dad. They got divorced, remember? Mum can't stand him and she can't stand me either because I'm exactly like him.' Lizzie let her hands drop. 'If she'd had her way I would have gone and lived with him. Neither of them wanted me.'

Amy felt her heart twist. 'Lizzie, I'm sure that isn't true.' She dropped onto her knees beside the bed and took the girl's hand. 'You and I are going to talk about that, but first we need to check you over to see why you've got this headache. When we've got the physical check out of the way, we'll deal with the rest of it.'

Lizzie rolled onto her back, her eyes closed. 'Go on, then. Get it over with. If I'm going to die, I might as well know.'

'You're not going to die, *angelo mia*.' As kind and gentle as he always was with little Michelle, Marco examined her thoroughly and closely checked the rash around her mouth. 'Amy, what exactly were you doing out with your friends last night?' His tone was casual as he put the stethoscope back into his bag and swiftly checked her blood pressure.

'I dunno.' Lizzie didn't open her eyes. 'We were just hanging out. Having fun. Drinking. You heard Mum.'

'What were you drinking?'

'Stuff.'

'Have you or your friends tried sniffing glue?'

Lizzie's eyes flew open and colour flooded into her face. 'No.'

'Lizzie.' Marco gently unwound the blood-pressure cuff and put it away, 'I'm your doctor, not your mother. You need to be honest with me.'

'Why? So that you can lecture me?'

'So that I can help you.'

Lizzie looked at him for a moment and then covered her face with her hands and started to cry again. 'They were doing it and I didn't want to be different. They're always saying I'm posh and stuck up. So I tried it. And I felt really happy and part of everything. And then afterwards I felt totally crap. Dizzy and sick. How did you guess?'

'I'm a doctor. And I suspected it when you came to the surgery last week. You were short-tempered, your mother mentioned that your school work had gone downhill and I noticed that you had an oil stain on your jumper.'

Lizzie gaped at him. 'What are you, a detective?'

'Sometimes, yes.' Marco gave a wry smile. 'That's exactly what my job is.'

'What about the spots on my face?'

'Same thing.'

Lizzie swallowed. 'Not meningitis?'

'Not meningitis,' Marco said gently. 'Glue sniffing.'

Lizzie groaned and closed her eyes. 'It's no big deal,' she muttered. 'I mean, I've only done it occasionally.'

'It *is* a big deal. Sometimes it can kill, sometimes it causes organ damage.' He talked to the teenager, dishing out cold, hard facts until Lizzie sat up and covered her ears with her hands.

'All right, stop! I've messed up, I know I have, but—you have no idea what it's like. Mum just *hates* me.' She started to cry again and Amy gave a murmur of sympathy and slid a hand over the girl's shaking shoulders.

'I don't think your mum hates you, Lizzie.'

'What would you know, anyway?' Lizzie wriggled away from her moodily. 'You, with your perfect life.'

'Actually, I know quite a lot about how it feels to be unloved,' Amy said calmly, 'because my mother didn't want me at all.'

Lizzie looked at her. So did Marco.

'Family life is complicated, Lizzie, but I know your mum loves you.' Amy's voice was firm. 'She's worried about you and she doesn't know how to handle you, but she loves you. All the signs are there.'

'What? She spends all her time with Michelle.'

Amy nodded. 'Yes, that must be hard. Michelle is a toddler

and toddlers are always time-consuming, and on top of that she has asthma. I can quite see how it might seem that your mum doesn't have time for you.'

'She doesn't even notice me except when it's to nag about something.'

'If she's nagging, then she's noticing,' Amy said quietly. 'My mother didn't care where I was or who I was with. When I was seven she sent me to boarding school. I would have given a great deal for her to nag me about something because at least it would have showed that she minded about something.'

Lizzie was silent. 'I hadn't thought of it like that.' She looked at Amy. 'We never talk or anything.'

'Do you talk to her?'

Lizzie's gaze slipped from hers. 'No.' She plucked at the duvet. 'I don't suppose I do. Not any more.'

'Then perhaps you should try. She might surprise you.'

Lizzie pulled a face. 'She's going to kill me when she finds out I've been sniffing glue. Are you going to tell her?'

'*You're* going to tell her,' Marco said gently, closing his bag, 'along with all these other things that you've been telling us. I think she needs to know how you feel, don't you?'

'It won't make a difference.'

'Why don't you tell her and we will find out?'

Lizzie curled her arms round her knees, suddenly looking very young and lost. 'Will you stay while I talk to her?'

Amy nodded immediately. 'I will.'

'I didn't really want to do it, you know? The glue stuff.' Lizzie's eyes filled. 'But those girls were like so cool and kind of superior and they look at you like you're *nothing* if you don't go along with what they say. I just wanted to fit in but at the same time I always knew that I didn't.'

'If they don't respect your right to make your own choices, maybe they're not good friends,' Amy said quietly, and Lizzie nodded.

'I know.' She wiped her nose on her sleeve. 'I think I just wanted Mum to notice me and when I hung out with them, Mum noticed. She hates them. So what happens now?'

'To start with, you talk to your mother. Hopefully she can give you the support you need.' Marco rose to his feet. 'If necessary I can refer you to the hospital for some help but I don't think you'll need it. Eat healthily, get plenty of sleep and let's see how you go. I'll go and call your mum.'

'Poor Lizzie. And poor Carol.' Marco drove towards home, a frown on his face.

'They'll be all right. They love each other and they'll work it out.' Amy glanced out of the window. 'Where are we going? This isn't the way home.'

'I want to talk to you.' He pulled up in a small car park that overlooked the jagged coastline. 'Here, we shouldn't be disturbed.'

Amy felt her heart sink. 'Marco, we're not going over this again.'

'No. We're exploring something entirely different. You are going to tell me about your childhood.'

'That's irrelevant. And it's not my favourite subject.'

'But you mentioned it just now to help a very confused, sad teenager. Doesn't our marriage deserve the same consideration?'

'Talking about the past won't make any difference to the future, Marco.'

'At least let me understand why you're walking away.' His voice was rough and his eyes were tired. 'At least give me that much, Amy. None of this makes sense to me. I'm sure that all your beliefs about marriage and children come from your own experiences. Clearly your mother didn't want children, but why does that affect your own perception of parenthood?'

'My mother *did* want children. But she wanted her own children.'

Marco was silent for a moment. 'This I don't understand.'

'I'm not her child,' Amy said wearily. 'I'm adopted, Marco. She adopted me because she was infertile and she couldn't have children. I was supposed to be the solution to her problem. Instead, I made the problem a thousand times worse.'

The only noise in the car was the sound of Marco breathing. 'You are adopted?'

'That's right. And now can we move on? There's really nothing else to say and it makes no difference to our relationship.'

'It makes a difference to me.' His voice was a low growl and he slid a hand behind her neck and forced her to look at him. '*Ti amo.* I love you. You love me.'

Amy swallowed and spoke with difficulty. 'That doesn't make a difference either.'

'How can you say that!' Visibly frustrated, his mouth tightened. 'Of course it's relevant. Our love is strong enough to survive anything.'

'No.' She shook her head. 'That isn't true. You want children. I can't give you children. I've seen firsthand what that can do to a relationship.'

'So tell me.' His voice was soft but the pressure of his hand prevented her from looking away. 'Tell me what it can do, I want to know. I want to know what you have seen that I am so blind to.'

'My father wanted children. My mother couldn't have them. So she adopted me, thinking that that would solve the problem. It didn't. My father never saw me as his and my mother blamed me for that. She believed that had I been different, he would have loved me.' Amy kept her voice level as she recited the basic facts. 'If I'd been prettier, cleverer, more outgoing—the list was endless. By the time she finally sent me to boarding school, I was so afraid of doing and saying the wrong thing, I barely spoke.'

'Amy.' Marco breathed her name and then gave a groan and pulled her against him. 'I had no idea. Why did you never tell me this before?'

'Because I try and forget it. I have a different life now. It isn't relevant.'

'If it's destroying our relationship, it's relevant. And your father paid you no attention either?'

'My father's ego was badly damaged by the lack of children. He thought it made him less of a man. He had an affair with his secretary and she became pregnant almost immediately. There was no question of keeping it a secret because my father wanted everyone to know that he'd fathered a child, as if it were somehow confirmation of his masculinity. So he divorced my mother and married the secretary. They had four children in quick succession, each one another bitter blow to my mother. I rarely ever saw her. During term time I was at school and in the holidays I stayed with my grandmother in Penhally.'

'I can't believe that she never tried to build a relationship with you.'

'You don't understand.' Amy gave a faint smile. 'She didn't really want me, Marco. I was just a solution to her problem. She needed to produce a child and she couldn't. So as a last resort she produced me. I'm sure the authorities would have thought that they were a perfect couple to qualify for adoption. Nice home, good income and my mother was very, very excited about having me. But not because she wanted me. Because she thought I'd save her marriage.'

'And when you didn't, she sent you away.'

'That's right.'

'So now I begin to understand you.' Marco stroked a hand

down her cheek. 'You think that perhaps I am like your father and I need children to prove my manhood, no?'

'I know you're nothing like my father.' She felt exhausted. And sick again, really, really sick. 'But I also know that you want a family and you deserve one.'

'Did your parents love each other?'

'Why is that relevant?'

'It's totally relevant.' His eyes held hers. 'You see, you are the one I want to spend my life with. And maybe our life together will come with problems, because life always does. Perhaps for us it will be infertility. But we will still be together and that is what I want. That is what I choose. A life with you.'

'Marco—'

'No, it is your turn to listen to me. All this time you have focused only on the fact you can't have children, not on our relationship.'

'Because it matters!'

'Of course it matters, I'm not pretending that it doesn't matter. I'm just saying that it can't be allowed to destroy what we have.'

'You don't understand—'

'No, *you* are the one who doesn't understand,' he said firmly. 'You don't understand how much I love you. If you understood that, you wouldn't ever think of leaving me again.'

'You really love me? Why?' Amy's eyes filled. 'I can't give you want you want.'

'Amy, *tesoro*.' He gave a gentle smile and lowered his mouth to hers. '*You* are what I want. How can I make you see that? I want my life to be with you and I will take whatever problems come along with that.'

She stared at him, her heart beating hard against her chest. 'We got married in a hurry.'

He gave a wry smile. 'Amy, I had successfully avoided

commitment for thirty-nine years until I met you. Are you seriously suggesting that I didn't know my own mind? I married you because you were the woman I wanted to spend the rest of my life with, and it took me very little time to work that out.'

'You said that you wanted me to be the mother of your children.'

He grimaced. '*Sì*. In the circumstances I can see how you would have arrived at your totally false belief that our marriage couldn't work. But what I was trying to say was that you were the only woman for me. The only woman I wanted to marry. The only woman I wanted to have children with.' His voice softened. 'Or not have children with, if that is what fate dictates for us. I love you.'

Amy stared at him, not daring to believe that he meant it. Then she felt her eyes fill. 'I didn't believe that you loved me.'

'I married you,' Marco said softly. 'Wasn't that proof enough of my love?'

'You didn't come after me when I left.'

He breathed out heavily. 'To begin with I was in shock. I couldn't believe what had happened because we went from being happy to you leaving in the blink of an eye. I would have come but then Annabel died and Nick needed me here. Time passed—'

'And I didn't come back because I just couldn't see how our relationship could survive. After everything I saw at home. Even now, I can't really believe that we can be different from my parents.'

'We *are* different. No two people are the same, remember that. And no relationship is the same. Have a little faith.' He brushed away her tears. 'If we weren't already married, this is the moment when I would propose. And you would say yes.'

'Would I?' She felt hope unfold inside her like the petals of a flower. 'What if—?'

'Life is full of what ifs. Let's deal just with what is. I love you. You love me. We stay together. And don't even think of arguing because I'm not going to listen. And don't think of leaving because I'll come after you.'

'Oh, Marco.' She flung her arms round his neck and felt his hand smooth her back.

'You are tired, *tesoro*. I need to take you home.'

'I love you.'

'I know. And I love you, too. And now you are going to rest because this has all been very traumatic for you. You are looking so, so tired at the moment.'

'It's probably just the worry. I've been dreading the thought of leaving you again.'

'You're not leaving. Not ever.'

'Do you mean it? You think everything can work?'

'I know it can.'

Amy leaned against him, feeling truly loved for the first time in her life. The feeling warmed her and she gave a soft smile.

If only she didn't feel so completely exhausted, everything about her life would be perfect.

The following morning Amy woke up with a churning stomach and only just made it to the bathroom before being violently sick.

'Amy?' Marco followed her into the bathroom, stroked her hair away from her face and then sat down on a chair and lifted her from the cold tiles onto his lap. 'Are you hot? Have you eaten something?'

'Obviously. Or maybe this is why I was so tired yesterday,' she murmured, sinking against his chest. 'I must have picked up a bug.'

'You weren't just tired yesterday,' Marco said gently. 'You are always tired.'

Amy felt a sudden flicker of unease. It was true. She *was* always tired.

What was the matter with her?

Was this another of life's cruel tricks? Had she finally found someone who truly loved her, only to become seriously ill?

'It's just a bug,' she said firmly. 'I feel better now I've been sick. I'll get dressed in a minute. We don't want to be late for surgery.'

'Don't be ridiculous. You can't take a surgery, feeling like this.'

She closed her eyes, wishing her stomach would settle. 'I'll be fine.'

'Amy.' Marco slid a hand over her forehead, checked her temperature and then gave her a smile. 'Spend the morning in bed. I'll be back to see you at lunchtime.'

She knew she ought to argue, but she just felt too tired to utter a protest so she allowed him to tuck her into bed and lay there, sleeping all morning until he reappeared.

'Do you feel any better?' He sat down on the bed next to her and stroked her face, his fingers cold from his short walk from the car. 'Have you been sick again?'

'No, just the once this morning.' She sat up. 'How was surgery?'

'Fine.' He hesitated. 'Amy, I'm going to say something and I hope you won't be upset.'

Her stomach dropped. 'You've changed your mind?'

'About what?' He looked baffled and she blushed.

'About spending your life with someone who can't have babies.'

His mouth tightened. 'I'm spending my life with you, that's what I want. But what I have to say does have to do with babies and I'm afraid you may misinterpret—' He broke off and let out a long breath. 'Amy, I want you to do a pregnancy test.'

'What?' She stared at him. 'Are you mad? Haven't you listened to a single thing I've said to you?'

'Look at your symptoms. Every day you're exhausted—'

'We're working hard!'

'You were sick this morning.'

'So? I've picked up a bug!' She pushed her hair away from her face and glared at him, her insides churning again. 'You're imagining it, Marco, just because you want it to happen. Wishful thinking. This is just what I was afraid of! You say it doesn't matter, *but it matters, Marco.* I can see that it matters to you.'

'No!' His voice was sharp. 'I knew this was going to be difficult because I knew you would make that association, but it isn't true. This isn't about our relationship. I'm a doctor, Amy, and I'm looking at your symptoms.'

'Well, you obviously haven't looked very closely because there's no way I…' Her voice tailed off and she looked at him. 'I can't be. You *know* I can't be.'

'I don't know that. I do know that fertility is an unpredictable thing. I know that we've been making love for almost a month now with no contraception.'

'I can't be pregnant!'

'Then do the test and we will know. Don't cry, please, don't cry.' He cursed softly and pulled her into his arms. *'Mi dispiace, tesoro.* Don't cry.'

Amy pulled away from him and wiped her hand over her face, furious with herself for being so emotional. What was happening to her? She'd never been the hysterical, weepy type. 'All right. I'll do it. Of course I'll do it if that's what you want me to do.' She sniffed and held out her hand. 'Do you have it?'

He hesitated and then reached into his jacket and pulled out the test. 'I'll come with you.'

She stared at the test in her hand. 'Would you mind if I did it on my own?' Her voice shook and he gave a sigh.

'Don't push me away, Amy. Don't push me away, *tesoro*. Not now when we are just learning how to share.'

Amy hesitated. She wasn't sure that she could actually do a pregnancy test in company, even when that company was Marco. 'The thing is,' she said honestly, 'even though I know it can't be positive, I want it to be, so badly. I—I just need a few moments…'

'I understand that.' Marco hugged her tightly. 'We'll compromise. Do the test and then call me.'

So that he could offer comfort.

And she was going to need comfort, she knew she was.

Amy closed the bathroom door and sat on the edge of the bath, the packet in her hand unopened. Why was she even hesitating? It wasn't as if she didn't know the answer, because she did. So why was she treating the test as if it were a bomb that was going to blow her life apart?

She didn't really think she was going to be pregnant, did she? Surely she wasn't really that stupid? *That delusional?* Had she really, somehow, allowed a tiny flicker of hope to creep in and contaminate her common sense?

With an impatient sound she stood up and unwrapped the test.

A few minutes later she was still staring at the stick, tears trickling unnoticed down her cheeks. The tiled bathroom floor was cold under her bare feet but she didn't notice that either.

'Amy?' His tone impatient and concerned by equal degrees, Marco pushed open the door without waiting for an invitation. 'Talk to me, *amore*. I'm sorry. I shouldn't have even suggested that you do that test. It was thoughtless of me and—'

'I'm pregnant.' Her voice was a hoarse whisper and she felt suddenly dizzy. 'Marco, I'm pregnant. I'm having our baby.'

She heard him swear softly and then felt his arms slide around her and support her as her legs gave way.

* * *

'So now I believe in happy endings.' Nick glanced between them and smiled. 'I'm pleased for you both. Really.'

Marco laughed in disbelief. 'I just told you that I want to leave the practice and return to Italy. It's not exactly a happy ending for you.'

Nick looked at him for a long moment and Amy saw something pass between the two men. An understanding. They'd shared so much. Loss. Pain. Pride at the way the practice had developed.

'Life moves on. Things change and we have to change with them.' Nick shrugged. 'We set this place up together and a lot of the success is down to you, Marco. The practice will go on without you. Grow. Change. I can understand that you and Amy want to go back to Italy.'

'Penhally will always remind Amy of her past.' Marco slid a protective arm around her and Amy looked up at him.

'And you miss Italy.'

'*Sì*. That is true.' He smiled at her. 'I miss Italy. I feel like the Maserati. In this weather, my engine suffers.'

'Well.' Nick cleared his throat. 'On a practical note, Adam Donnelly is due to start tomorrow, as you know, so we won't be left high and dry.'

'We can stay for a few months if that would help.'

Nick shook his head. 'I don't want you to do that. You've managed to sort things out and I'm pleased about that. You've no idea how pleased. Now I want you to go and get on with your lives. Get ready for that baby.'

'You're very generous.' Marco's voice was gruff. 'Thank you.'

'*Prego*. Isn't that what I'm supposed to say?'

'And what about you, my friend?'

A shadow flickered in Nick's eyes. 'I carry on building the practice. Supporting the community. Kate's resigned.'

'Oh, no!' Despite the conversation they'd had, Amy

couldn't help feeling shocked. She hadn't actually believed that Kate would do it.

'And you accepted her resignation?' Marco's gaze was steady and Amy held her breath. It was the nearest any of them had come to asking Nick directly about his relationship with Kate.

'It's disappointing for the practice but she wants to take a new direction in her career. It would be wrong of me to talk her out of it.'

Work. He only talked about work. Nothing personal. *Nothing about missing Kate or feeling anything for Kate.*

For a moment Amy was tempted to step forward and shake him. Didn't he know how Kate felt about him? And was he really pretending that he felt nothing for Kate? She knew that wasn't true. Not after the scene she'd witnessed on New Year's Eve.

'Nick—'

'People are complicated,' Marco said quietly, closing his hand over Amy's to silence her. 'Relationships are complicated. And not all the obstacles to happiness come from outside and can be solved. Sometimes they are inside us and only time can shift them.'

For a moment Nick didn't respond. 'And sometimes time just isn't enough. Good luck, the two of you. Stay in touch. I look forward to holidays in Italy.'

They walked away from the surgery and Marco turned to look back.

'You're going to miss it, aren't you?' Amy slid her hand into his and he turned and smiled at her.

'I'm ready to move on. Do something else. I suppose I feel a little guilty about leaving Nick, especially as Kate is leaving, too. Whatever is going on between them, she has been a big part of the Penhally Bay Surgery for a long time.'

'She would have stayed if he'd told her that he loved her.'

'Nick has far too many issues after Annabel's death. He isn't ready to think about another relationship. Perhaps he never will be.'

Amy sighed. 'Why didn't you make him admit that he is in love with Kate?'

'I'm not sure that he knows it himself. And I'm not a doctor of relationships.'

Amy slipped her arm into his. 'I think you are. You cured ours. I can't believe this has happened. I arrived in Penhally a month ago to ask you to give me a divorce and now here I am back with you and pregnant. It's like a dream.'

'But a good dream.'

'Of course.' She reached up and kissed him. 'It's like being given a second chance. When I first met you I was so in love and then it all went so wrong. I didn't believe our relationship could work if I was infertile because I'd seen what it did to my parents.'

'It isn't about fertility, it's about love. Your parents didn't share the love that we have for each other.'

'No. I think you're right about that.'

'You know I'm right.' He slid his arms around her waist. 'I'm always right.'

'And so modest. So what happens now?'

'We make our home in Italy. The sun will put some colour in your cheeks and you will grow so accustomed to being loved that there will be no room for doubt in your mind. And you will speak Italian and learn how to make pasta from scratch.'

Amy laughed. 'And Penhally?'

He glanced around him, his eyes warm. 'This place has been a part of our lives. But it's time to move on.' His gaze moved back to hers. 'Will you move on with me, *tesoro*? Build a new life? Do you trust me enough to give up everything you know?'

'Yes.' She answered without hesitation. 'The only thing I don't want to give up is you. You're all that matters.'

Marco gave a slow smile of satisfaction. 'Finally, we agree on something.'

And he bent his head and kissed her.

MILLS & BOON

Pure reading pleasure

NOVEMBER 2007 HARDBACK TITLES

ROMANCE

The Italian Billionaire's Ruthless Revenge *Jacqueline Baird*	978 0 263 19716 7
Accidentally Pregnant, Conveniently Wed *Sharon Kendrick*	978 0 263 19717 4
The Sheikh's Chosen Queen *Jane Porter*	978 0 263 19718 1
The Frenchman's Marriage Demand *Chantelle Shaw*	978 0 263 19719 8
The Millionaire's Convenient Bride *Catherine George*	978 0 263 19720 4
Expecting His Love-Child *Carol Marinelli*	978 0 263 19721 1
The Greek Tycoon's Unexpected Wife *Annie West*	978 0 263 19722 8
The Italian's Captive Virgin *India Grey*	978 0 263 19723 5
Her Hand in Marriage *Jessica Steele*	978 0 263 19724 2
The Sheikh's Unsuitable Bride *Liz Fielding*	978 0 263 19725 9
The Bridesmaid's Best Man *Barbara Hannay*	978 0 263 19726 6
A Mother in a Million *Melissa James*	978 0 263 19727 3
The Rancher's Doorstep Baby *Patricia Thayer*	978 0 263 19728 0
Moonlight and Roses *Jackie Braun*	978 0 263 19729 7
Their Miracle Child *Gill Sanderson*	978 0 263 19730 3
Single Dad, Nurse Bride *Lynne Marshall*	978 0 263 19731 0

HISTORICAL

The Vanishing Viscountess *Diane Gaston*	978 0 263 19778 5
A Wicked Liaison *Christine Merrill*	978 0 263 19779 2
Virgin Slave, Barbarian King *Louise Allen*	978 0 263 19780 8

MEDICAL™

The Italian's New-Year Marriage Wish *Sarah Morgan*	978 0 263 19824 9
The Doctor's Longed-For Family *Joanna Neil*	978 0 263 19825 6
Their Special-Care Baby *Fiona McArthur*	978 0 263 19826 3
A Family for the Children's Doctor *Dianne Drake*	978 0 263 19827 0

Pure reading pleasure

1007 Gen Std LP

NOVEMBER 2007 LARGE PRINT TITLES

ROMANCE

Bought: The Greek's Bride *Lucy Monroe*	978 0 263 19495 1
The Spaniard's Blackmailed Bride *Trish Morey*	978 0 263 19496 8
Claiming His Pregnant Wife *Kim Lawrence*	978 0 263 19497 5
Contracted: A Wife for the Bedroom *Carol Marinelli*	978 0 263 19498 2
The Forbidden Brother *Barbara McMahon*	978 0 263 19499 9
The Lazaridis Marriage *Rebecca Winters*	978 0 263 19500 2
Bride of the Emerald Isle *Trish Wylie*	978 0 263 19501 9
Her Outback Knight *Melissa James*	978 0 263 19502 6

HISTORICAL

Dishonour and Desire *Juliet Landon*	978 0 263 19409 8
An Unladylike Offer *Christine Merrill*	978 0 263 19410 4
The Roman's Virgin Mistress *Michelle Styles*	978 0 263 19411 1

MEDICAL™

A Bride for Glenmore *Sarah Morgan*	978 0 263 19371 8
A Marriage Meant To Be *Josie Metcalfe*	978 0 263 19372 5
Dr Constantine's Bride *Jennifer Taylor*	978 0 263 19373 2
His Runaway Nurse *Meredith Webber*	978 0 263 19374 9
The Rescue Doctor's Baby Miracle *Dianne Drake*	978 0 263 19547 7
Emergency at Riverside Hospital *Joanna Neil*	978 0 263 19548 4

1107 Gen Std HB

MILLS & BOON
Pure reading pleasure

DECEMBER 2007 HARDBACK TITLES

ROMANCE

The Greek Tycoon's Defiant Bride *Lynne Graham*	978 0 263 19732 7
The Italian's Rags-to-Riches Wife *Julia James*	978 0 263 19733 4
Taken by Her Greek Boss *Cathy Williams*	978 0 263 19734 1
Bedded for the Italian's Pleasure *Anne Mather*	978 0 263 19735 8
The Sheikh's Virgin Princess *Sarah Morgan*	978 0 263 19736 5
The Virgin's Wedding Night *Sara Craven*	978 0 263 19737 2
Innocent Wife, Baby of Shame *Melanie Milburne*	978 0 263 19738 9
The Sicilian's Ruthless Marriage Revenge *Carole Mortimer*	978 0 263 19739 6
Cattle Rancher, Secret Son *Margaret Way*	978 0 263 19740 2
Rescued by the Sheikh *Barbara McMahon*	978 0 263 19741 9
Her One and Only Valentine *Trish Wylie*	978 0 263 19742 6
English Lord, Ordinary Lady *Fiona Harper*	978 0 263 19743 3
The Playboy's Plain Jane *Cara Colter*	978 0 263 19744 0
Executive Mother-To-Be *Nicola Marsh*	978 0 263 19745 7
A Single Dad at Heathermere *Abigail Gordon*	978 0 263 19746 4
The Sheikh Surgeon's Proposal *Olivia Gates*	978 0 263 19747 1

HISTORICAL

A Compromised Lady *Elizabeth Rolls*	978 0 263 19781 5
Runaway Miss *Mary Nichols*	978 0 263 19782 2
My Lady Innocent *Annie Burrows*	978 0 263 19783 9

MEDICAL™

The Doctor's Bride By Sunrise *Josie Metcalfe*	978 0 263 19828 7
Found: A Father For Her Child *Amy Andrews*	978 0 263 19829 4
Her Very Special Baby *Lucy Clark*	978 0 263 19830 0
The Heart Surgeon's Secret Son *Janice Lynn*	978 0 263 19831 7

1107 Gen Std LP

Pure reading pleasure

DECEMBER 2007 LARGE PRINT TITLES

ROMANCE

Taken: the Spaniard's Virgin *Lucy Monroe*	978 0 263 19503 3
The Petrakos Bride *Lynne Graham*	978 0 263 19504 0
The Brazilian Boss's Innocent Mistress	978 0 263 19505 7
Sarah Morgan	
For the Sheikh's Pleasure *Annie West*	978 0 263 19506 4
The Italian's Wife by Sunset *Lucy Gordon*	978 0 263 19507 1
Reunited: Marriage in a Million *Liz Fielding*	978 0 263 19508 8
His Miracle Bride *Marion Lennox*	978 0 263 19509 5
Break Up to Make Up *Fiona Harper*	978 0 263 19510 1

HISTORICAL

No Place For a Lady *Louise Allen*	978 0 263 19412 8
Bride of the Solway *Joanna Maitland*	978 0 263 19413 5
Marianne and the Marquis *Anne Herries*	978 0 263 19414 2

MEDICAL™

Single Father, Wife Needed *Sarah Morgan*	978 0 263 19375 6
The Italian Doctor's Perfect Family	978 0 263 19376 3
Alison Roberts	
A Baby of Their Own *Gill Sanderson*	978 0 263 19377 0
The Surgeon and the Single Mum *Lucy Clark*	978 0 263 19378 7
His Very Special Nurse *Margaret McDonagh*	978 0 263 19549 1
The Surgeon's Longed-For Bride	978 0 263 19550 7
Emily Forbes